The Murder Boys

John B Bliss

CRIME WAVE PRESS

One
THROWING THINGS AT TRAINS

It started with a slippery little bit of clay. It spat out between George Dukes' plump little fingers and landed on my cheek. I turned to look at George but he was too busy trying to roll and didn't look up. I could feel the wet clay tighten on my face and, as it dried in the sun, I knew it was time for the scuffle. Blake, George's elder brother, had been niggling away at Ali all afternoon. I thought if I started on George, Blake might leave Ali alone. I sent a challenge ringing across the nook to George. "Watch what you're doing, lardy cake."

George looked up sharply, hurt, confused by my insult out of nowhere. He stared at me, his jaw tightened and his dark eyes narrowed as he brooded on the insult. But he soon bit. "Shut up," he muttered, "where's your dad?"

That was all I needed. I got to my feet. "What did you say?"

George sneered. "I said where's your dad? You heard me."

I fell on him, pinning his arms either side of him, pushing him back towards the rail tracks. He kicked out viciously and I felt his knee hard in my chest. Suddenly my breath was all gone and I toppled back towards the centre of the nook, away from the tracks. I heard Blake laugh out loud and then felt George's oily fists jarring round my cheekbones and temples. The best he had. And not enough. I recovered and jumped him again, going in close under his fists and gripping his sweaty torso hard. In the dust, I rolled him over onto his

3

front, kneading his soft body like warm dough. Then I had him trapped underneath me, his fists all tangled up and useless. Of course, me lying on top of him, that was all comedy for the audience. I heard Blake hoot again, loving it. But I knew that even though Blake might be laughing, he would be watching carefully. He might kick me off any time, look after his little George.

My nose was right in George's hair. I was getting an extreme close-up of his dirty grey skin and a load of dandruff. It reminded me of something you'd see in a museum, the hide of some dusty, stuffed animal: a mole, a cat or a chimpanzee.

Then, inch by inch, I began to work my left arm out from beneath George's tubby body until it was free to tap at his head. Knock knock. Give Up. Fat man. Give up. George stank (margarine, dirty laundry, sweat and milk) but I didn't care. The only thing here was to win the fight.

George shifted his weight a fraction and my right hand freed up too. Now I could reach up and push hard at his chin, bend his neck right back. I was winning! And a song of victory arrived. *We are the champions, no time for losers 'cos we are the champions.* He shouted out, tried kicking out again, but my legs were wrapped around his, strangling his limbs like bindweed. Our bodies were oozing sweat; I could feel George's moisture, salty tears and grease, wringing through my fingers. He was finished, gasping for air.

"Give up." My voice, a ridiculous pipsqueak, terrible.

George growled and made a last attempt to force himself free. I held the tension in his shoulders and back and pushed back harder against his neck. I heard Blake's boots shift in the grass; he let something loose, a cough or maybe a snigger.

"Alright, alright let go." George was reduced to nothing and I felt a bit of sadness for him. But not that much.

"Give up?"

"Yeah. Just let go will you."

I hauled myself off him, leaving him panting and broken

in the dust. The sad little clay balls he had been making were crushed. Blake looked me up and down, making his assessment, looking at his new third place. He took in the sweat on my T-shirt, my ruffled hair and my crumpled cheeks, and calculated my worth. He didn't think I would win, I thought with satisfaction. I was bigger, or at least taller, than George, and older too, but still he thought his brother would have it. He thought he had kicked enough guts into George to see off a posh like me.

"Six balls Rich?"

The thing with Blake, he was always surprising you. I had just defeated his younger brother and claimed third place. And all he wanted to hear about is how many damn clay balls I had made.

"Six," I admitted.

I tried to avoid Blake's eyes. I looked at the walls of the nook behind him instead: chalk walls, brambles, cascading ivy, slates of sunlight. When I did look at him, his gaze had shifted; I watched it take in Ali's respectable eight and the wreckage of George's efforts before coming to rest thoughtfully on the twelve perfect specimens he had produced.

George picked himself up off the floor, face crimson, tears lining his olive eye cavities. He was muttering little threats. "Bastard you are. Nearly broke my neck."

I set my features hard. "More?"

He looked at the floor. No.

Ali jumped in, a good number two, and told me to leave it, and then Blake raised a hand and looked suddenly alert and attentive. "Train," he said.

We moved into the buddleia at the back of the nook, as far from the tracks as possible. In there was a damp, earthy little den about the size of a phone box on its side. The top two rolled in before me and then George squeezed in at the end, smelling softly of defeat.

The train was a magnificent thing. First the nose, all yellow paint and lethal coupling; next, the driver's cabin, a blur of glass, a bit reflective so you could sort of see the driver, his cap and his fag. Last you got the carriages. Flash-frames: men in pinstripe staring like idiots at nothing; families eating pork pies; stuff like that. Then as suddenly as it had arrived, the train was gone, and we were left standing in silence again.

Somewhere, a wood pigeon cooed. Blake pushed the buddleia branches aside and stepped back into the nook. He looked again at the three primitive piles of clay balls. "Clay'll dry out," he said, as if to himself.

"Yeah," said Ali, "be like chucking rocks, could break the windows."

Blake wasn't impressed with that. Ignoring Ali, he headed off towards the nook's far corner and pulled a plastic bag out of his jacket pocket. In there was a squashed, sweaty cheese sandwich. He threw it to George and shook the crumbs out of the bag and examined it for holes. We were all standing watching him, not knowing what to do or what he was going to do next. "Rich," he said. And my heart skipped because here it comes, I thought, my punishment for beating up his brother. But no, he was pointing at the brambles round the edge of the nook.

"We'll need the water in there."

"What?" It was really thorny, full of nettles too. At the back of it all there was some dirty puddle. It was a punishment all right.

"Get us some of that."

Ali tried to help me. "But how can he…?"

Blake stared him down, really hard, like Ali was some idiot. "Like this," he said. Then, grabbing hold of a bit of buddleia, he flexed it until the bark split. Once he had it, he used it like a giant fan to attack the brambles, following up with his boots until he had cleared a path leading to the water. He got there, cupped his hands, collected a handful and let a little drain between his fingers for us to see. He knew our eyes were on

6

him. He dribbled a bit into the sandwich bag then headed back towards us at the centre of the nook, picked up one of his balls of clay and added it to the bag. Finally he tied the whole thing up and gave it a gentle shake. You had to hand it to him: it was the work of a genius. That sweaty sandwich bag now had the feel and weight of a beanbag. It would be truly lovely to throw.

Blake tossed the bag lightly to Ali, and carried on speaking to him like he was stupid. "You throw it, from here."

Ali's face fell. Now he was being punished for doubting our leader's authority. He pointed towards the tracks and started stammering all over the place.

"But...what will I...I can't just..."

"Don't matter. You stay out of sight till the driver's gone, then you run out and you do it." Blake sneered nastily, enjoying the moment. "Cover your face if you want but it's only the passengers what'll see you."

"Train," said George.

He wasn't wrong. That sea-sicky clitter-clatter was starting again. The Dukes bolted for cover and we followed, crouching in the cool. Ali was right beside me, nearest the exit. I could hear his breath, fast and hard even over the bloody din of the train. I glanced sideways at him, fearful for him but glad as hell it wasn't me who had to run out and attack this train.

The express hit the clearing. Suddenly everything was all hurtling steel and rushing colour. Blake reached behind me to push Ali hard in the small of the back.

"Go."

And Ali leapt out! Covering his face like a bandit with one side of his jacket and holding the saggy bag with his right hand, he advanced to the position that Blake had told him to take and, without hesitation, launched his missile at the train. The bag exploded on impact; it made a glorious splat, a perfect circle, like a massive cow pat on its side.

We watched in wonder as Ali turned away from the train, the glory of victory on his face.

Two

JESUS CHRIST

On the way home, we stopped at the junction of St Margaret's Road and Kingston Road to look at the Jesus statue outside the church. Spread onto his grey plaster cross, the son of God stared desperately back at us. I liked to look at the way the nails had been driven through his hands and feet and imagined the pain the poor bloke was in. The sculptor had had a lot of fun, daubing blood enthusiastically around the nails and then adding lovely little red rivers running down the face and into his beard from his crown of thorns. We paused in silent contemplation.

"Good shot today," I said.

"Thanks," said Ali, "lucky though."

"Still. Good one."

Ali was a proper good kid. A lot of other people would be bragging about what he had done. But while he knew that he had been brave and was a bit of a hero now, he also knew he had only done it because he had to, a bit like a soldier really, just getting on with the war.

Then a filthy old greyhound was about us, all grizzled and grey, with one of those little bellies you could get your thumb and forefinger round, sniffing away at our crotches. We had been so absorbed in our thoughts and the crucified Jesus that we hadn't realised we were not alone. At the side of the church, sprawled out on the public benches were three men and a woman. They had been looking at us the whole time, laughing silent as we gawped at the Christ and when we looked up they all started cackling heartily. In the middle was Shanklin, a navy cap squeezed over black murder eyes and a barrel chest full of grog. Squeezed next to him, Tim Physics, a ghost, practically dead. He was a student, astrophysics genius, but nearly gone. And Mary Sullivan, a spiteful red-faced Irish woman who, rumour had it, lost her husband and child in a house fire. Together they were a terrifyingly ugly family, showing us their drunken toothless gobs.

The greyhound's owner stood apart from the others. Wild Bill, rake thin in snakeskin boots, straggle beard and a wide-brimmed leather cowboy hat pulled down to just above his eyes. Maybe an American who grew up on a cattle ranch, maybe a bullshitting alcoholic, probably both. Blake insisted his dad knew him, or knew him once, and he was what he claimed to be, a proper cowboy who had somehow lost his Wild West. I was sceptical but I kept that to myself. As we looked up at him, he turned his lazy gaze from the drunken middle distance and squinted in our direction, finally focusing on his dog. "Injuns, Belle," he called out, letting his bottle fall limply to his side, "Injun boys. Bad medicine." His drinking companions gave us another round of mocking laughter, and, not knowing what else to do, we grinned back at them like half-wits.

Finally they got bored and went back to their bottles. I said cheerio to Ali on the corner of Juxon Street, ambled down the road, opened a side gate, dropped six feet down some steps and appeared at my open back door. Sausages spat in mum's pan. My two-year-old sister Rachel shouted nonsense at me and strained at the harness in her high chair. Her face was always a mess, covered in spit and churned up food. Mum lowered a basket of uncooked chips into a deep fat fryer. Home.

"Had a good day?" Sometimes Mum looked young, a bit of a hippy, carefree, and sometimes she looked full of worry.

It wasn't easy of course: dad gone and the three of us on her hands. Anyway on that day she looked fine, cheerful. She handed Rachel another finger of bread and gave me one of her friendly but scrutinising smiles, wiping her hands on her apron.

"Yeah. Good."

"Where have you been?"

"Nowhere."

"Nowhere?"

"On the meadow and playing football a bit."

"We were at the park earlier, weren't we Rachel?" She looked at my baby sister like she expected her to answer but Rachel had already turned the bread and her spit into an oozy toy, letting the pulp squidge deliciously between her fingers. "We didn't see you there." Still keeping on.

TV music struck up and I tried to make a move. She pinned me down with her kind eye stare.

"Who were you with?"

"Ali, and some others, I don't know."

"The Dukes boys?"

The inquisition. Why was she asking? What did she know? "No. I think they're away somewhere. Mum, you got any sandwich bags?"

"Sandwich bags? Somewhere probably." Her brow all creased up. "What do you want them for?"

"Nothing. Just wondered. I'm watching telly."

I tried to get away again but she pointed to some salad ingredients she'd laid out. "Will you make your dressing?"

I was willing to do that if she stopped asking me questions. I reached for the small blue jug from above the cooker and a teaspoon from a drawer beside the sink and gave myself over to the rhythms of the kitchen. Three teaspoons of olive oil and one of vinegar. I heard mum chop the lettuce and gather it into a salad shaker. I whisked the mixture vigorously with the teaspoon. Mum threw in peppers, tomatoes and cucumbers after the lettuce. The shaker whirled, Rachel gurgled, the oil and vinegar thickened. No one said anything; it was pretty nice.

Mum served up and my older sister Beth arrived. Beth spent those days waiting for her A-level results to hit the doormat, lying around in front of the TV. When she was off the sofa, she drank coffee with her goth girlfriends. They had let their enormous hair grow wild and whispered in tired and cynical drawls – they were boring as hell and completely annoying. She sat herself down grudgingly at the table with mum and me and, refusing a sausage, settled for a large plate of salad and a few chips. We picked over our meal as Rachel gleefully chucked handfuls of bread pulp at the wall.

"Where do tramps actually sleep?" From me, out before I could think about it.

Beth looked up wearily, "I didn't realise it was non-sequitur week."

Secateurs? Non-secateurs? Beth spoke a foreign tongue, designed specifically to confuse me. I had no idea what anything she said actually meant. Mum decided my question might deserve some sort of logical response. "Well there's a shelter in St Aldates," she explained, "some of them sleep there but some of them…I don't know. Anywhere they can find I suppose."

"How do they get money?"

"I don't know," Mum tossed a little of my dressing across her leaves. "Perhaps social security or maybe they work here and there. I think the church helps some of them."

"Even Wild Bill?"

"Oh my God." Beth looked up from the pile of salad she had been toying with.

"Who the hell is Wild Bill?"

"The cowboy at the church. With the hat."

"My brother is insane," sighed Beth. And then Rachel brought the whole thing to a halt by tipping her plastic bowl of shredded sausages and chips onto the floor. Thank God for that.

Three

WILD BILL

And out of that plastic bag filled with clay goo the whole thing grew. I found the sandwich bags and with them, we could properly go to work manufacturing ammunition. The missiles amassed in front of us: glassy white plastic sandwich bags with Blake's patented clay and water mix inside, laid out all limp and stranded like dead fish on the grass. All four of us worked hard: each gathering a clutch of milky clay, rolling it into balls and gently shaking little missiles into life.

Time went awry in the nook, ghosting, twisting and distorting. We worked mainly in a grog sun hush but, like Quasimodo's demented bells, the roar of the trains kept shattering the silence, reminding us of our purpose. Four trains had gone through, two hours had passed. Maybe. In any case, we had enough bombs; we were ready to try out our ammunition.

We were dressed right too. I had my mum's green silk headscarf tied cowboy style around my neck, ready to raise and tuck over my nose bandana style. Ali wore his trademark white, blue and yellow Leeds United scarf with the Dukes black woollen balaclavas pushed over their gleaming sweaty foreheads in stand-by mode.

"Here we go," Blake murmured.

He was right: the old ratter tatter was beginning again. Our stomachs jumped and retched in time to the beat. Blake pulled his balaclava down. Now he was a grainy TV terrorist. George copied his brother, but somehow he managed to look like a battered teddy bear instead. Ali pulled his scarf tight over his mouth, like a WW2 pilot about to jump into his cockpit. The incoming train was howling like the whistle of a boiling kettle. I pulled the green silk over my nose and mouth. In the gathering noise, we steeled ourselves for the battle.

The southbound express hit the nook, a rush of air and noise, its red and blue striped nose ate up the gap between the nook's sides in seconds. I glimpsed a black-capped driver at the controls.

"Go! Go! Go!"

Blake's woollen head screaming orders at us. George and I mesmerised by the noise and rush of stale summer air. Ali gone. He was at his pile. Blake broken cover too, pulling roughly at my shoulder as he bounded out of the bush. He seized a missile. Ali's arm drew back and, arching forward, he released his bag with venom. The faces of startled passengers as they came under attack: a young girl with blonde pigtails, her mouth opening in stunned disbelief; an old man pointing incredulously. Then Blake obliterated the old man's image in a circular splat of clay followed by George's first hit, the air now thick with projectiles as the other three let fly with all their might. Me standing frozen in the midst of the carnage, so hypnotised by the frenzy around me, I had forgotten my duties. I reached down and lobbed my first bag; it traveled in a lazy loop and burst at the top of a window filled with the indignant faces of men in pinstripe suits. Amazing. I was laughing, I think. The possibility of wetting my trousers. Pissing myself laughing: before that moment I had heard it but never felt it. I threw another bomb and this time it hit the centre of a window fractionally before someone else's, a superb double splatter.

And then, as suddenly as it arrived, the train was gone and we were left blinking in the silence of the nook. George tore his balaclava off, his face crimson with heat. Someone began to laugh but then thought better of it.

"Time to go," said Blake. "See you at the camp." He grabbed George's sleeve and tugged his brother back towards the line. Ali and I were left at the crime scene. That wood pigeon started cooing again.

"I don't see why we have to go that way," said Ali, looking right along the tracks, in the opposite direction from the Duke boys' retreat.

"Me neither."

That's where we did it, questioned his orders for the first time. Ali looked relieved. "We could wait here for a bit then go that way as well," he suggested, nodding to our left.

"Trouble is… if they see us…" I didn't need to spell out the consequences of disobeying instructions. "And if we stay…"

"Someone might come," Ali said, "Probably will."

"Definitely will. Did you see them? On the train." We shared a grin as we thought of the shocked and startled passengers' faces as the clay bombs rained down on them. I moved towards the south exit of the nook. "C'mon, let's just do it."

The track stretched ahead. In the distance, we could see the sky blue iron of the sides of the rail bridge but with the heat shimmers it was hard to gauge how far away it was. Beside the tracks, dock leaves were sprouting out from the gravel but they weren't going to provide any cover if a train came through. It got worse. The greenery gave way to a hundred-yard stretch of sheer chalk walls. We legged through it, anxious not to be caught. Eventually the clay walls stooped and disappeared in impenetrable thorny bramble on one side of the track.

"Ali," I said, "I think I hear a train." We stopped.

"Jesus!" Ali stepped away from the track and looked anxiously each way. Then he saw me grinning at him, shook his head and flashed a smile. "Idiot."

"Run," I shouted out and set off towards the bridge, pelting down the middle of the tracks. I could hear Ali's trainers hitting the sleepers behind me and I opened up my lungs and screamed. "Jesus! Jesus H Christ!"

"Jesus H!" yelled Ali in reply. "Jesus H Christ!"

We got to the bridge just as a northbound appeared in the distance and vaulted over the bridge's side, dropping down onto the footpath that ran under the tracks.

"You're supposed to go that way," I said, pointing towards the canal.

"Go where I bloody like. Hitler. Who does he think he is?" Away from him, Blake's influence was weaker. We were chipping away at his authority.

"What if we left the gang?"

"We'd have to fight him," Ali said.. "We couldn't just leave."

"Well we can't run away from him either. So we'll do what he says for now but if he starts on either of us, we've got to stick up for each other, right?"

Ali smiled. "Yeah that's right. He can't take the two of us."

"George?"

"What about him? Fat bastard." We were laughing but we weren't really sure. Neither of us knew whether together were really capable of winning a two against two.

I left Ali at the towpath and headed back towards the camp. Ali headed away from the canal, setting off on a wide arc through the meadow that would take him to the camp a different way. Half a mile of filthy old canal and then I made out a dog ahead and soon realised it was Belle, coiled in front of Wild Bill's cowboy boots in an obedient heap. There he was, bottle in hand, staring morosely out at the iron foundry on the other side of the canal, his wide-brimmed hat pulled over his eyes. I softened my step, hoping I might pass unnoticed. No chance of that. As I approached, Belle looked up sniffing and Bill, in the process of bringing the bottle to his lips, brought it back down again. He looked at me coolly as I advanced towards him up the towpath.

"You're a clay soldier," he began, steady, testing, a trace of menace in his voice. I stopped dead in my tracks and he drank up my reaction, enjoying me looking foolish. Then he began to chuckle to himself, spat carefully on the ground beside him, cleared his throat and took a big swig from his bottle. "Sit down," he said, patting the seat beside him. "Sit down little injun." I opened my mouth but his watery eyes had me pinned. "Don't say you can't 'cos you can." He sang softly like an uncle to a favourite nephew, pushed the brim of his hat away from his eyes and I stared as the watery brown irises opened and contracted around the bottomless black well of his pupils. "I'm not so stupid as I look so don't treat me so," he said. Beaten, I sat down next to him on the bench.

Close up Bill reeked of stale booze, sweat and the sickly tar of cigarettes. From a distance, he might have been some kind of eccentric individual, maybe a circus performer or pop singer. But as I sat next to him there was no doubt as to what and who Wild Bill was. The felt of his hat was limp and worn, his jeans shone with grease and his boots were scuffed and shapeless.

"I've seen you today little injun," he said, flashing a smile from behind a mottled beard, revealing several missing teeth. "You've been out on the railroads with your injun gang. What you been doing there I wonder?"

"Nothing much."

"Really. Nothing much. Is that a fact." Bill turned questions into statements, the fake friendly style teachers used when they wanted information. Bill took a pull of his sherry and brought it up in front of me, holding it there for a second or two as if offering it for my inspection. A yellow label, VP. I didn't mind a bit of sherry actually and had slugged at mum's Christmas bottle for the last couple of years, but the idea of sharing anything with Bill was utterly disgusting. Anyway I needn't have worried: he wasn't going to let me have any of his precious booze. He soon replaced the cap and deposited the bottle beside the bench on the ground. "I saw a train come past the bridge there," he said, pointing towards the sky blue metal in the distance, "Covered in clay it was, covered in clay." More searching looks but I couldn't tell whether Bill was really confused by the muddy train or knew precisely how this had come about. I decided on silence. We simply stared at one another. I realised that to leave I would have to humour him, to play cowboys and Indians with Bill. I tore my eyes away from his stare and scrambled to my feet.

"I can't stay. I don't know about the train, Mr. Bill," I stammered, performing a terrified ragamuffin for him. Bill grinned heartily, loving the theatre of it. Then, back in role as a stern inquisitor, he stared at me evenly, waiting for me to retract my statement, but I carried on, still acting my part. "I hope you enjoy being a cowboy again when you go back to that life, Bill, we all wish you well in that."

Bill's lips broke open into a gaping grin. Then he began to shake with silent mirth as he struggled to control himself. His pinched frame rattled as raucous laughter began to escape from his lips and finally he guffawed and cackled as he slapped the greasy denim of his thighs and wiped tears of blind joy from his face. I walked away, Wild Bill's demented laughter ringing in my ears.

Four

GEORGE DUKES

The camp, our camp, two rotting armchairs and a sofa pulled into a hedge in the middle of the town tip, shrouded in dirty afternoon shadows. But it was still hot. I arrived flustered and covered in sweat. Immediately I sensed something was out of place, but I couldn't work out what it was.

"Rich, where you been?" Blake from his place in the best chair. King Blake on his throne.

"Nowhere. I saw Wild Bill."

"So?" He had gone all confrontational, cold. I noticed then what was wrong: George was in Ali's chair, the number two's chair. The fat boy looked comfortable too, armed with a stash of little pebbles ready to chuck at an old can he had arranged at the edge of the clearing. He leered at me; yesterday's clash was not forgotten.

"He was asking me about the train."

"What about it?" Blake was trying to trap me. "What did you say?"

"Nothing." The brothers were looking at me nasty.

A rustle behind me and Ali was there. He noticed George straight away. "You're in my chair," he muttered.

Blake licked his lips and switched his attention to George who ignored Ali and chucked one of his little pebbles casually at his can. It missed and he swore softly. Ali was still behind me but I could smell his anger. The air was all close and humid; George was looking to wind him up, provoke a reaction.

He got one.

"Get up." The ugliness in the camp's air was building: violence, hatred, and frustration all swimming round us like piranhas. I glanced at Blake. A smile ghosted his lips, he was looking forward to this. I realised he had set the situation up and I was suddenly frightened for Ali. George tossed another stone at the can. This time, it struck true with a clear ring ding.

"Make me."

Ali bustled past me, knocking my arm out of the way, and I felt the tension, the anger in him. He crossed the clearing and headed straight for George. There was no doubt in my mind that George would get a mauling but I could see what Ali couldn't, the trap doors opening up. I could see the violence that would unfold because this time Blake would step in. But I didn't stop it. I couldn't.

Too fired up, too impulsive, Ali reached out to get hold of George's shoulder and pull him to the floor. But George was ready, he planted a Doc Martin into Ali's stomach. Ali staggered backwards, winded, gasping for air and suddenly George was on his feet. The podgy boy was suddenly all elegance and poise. His right fist coiled and struck hard and true on Ali's left ear. And he then he took his moment: he turned like a dancer and stamped precisely and viciously on Ali's foot. I had seen something like that on the Saturday afternoon wrestling; it was pretty impressive to watch, I had to admit. Ali starting howling in pain and confusion, undone by George's fighting skills. I moved to help my friend but then I felt my upper arm encased in iron, the vice of Blake's grip. Blake had moved to stand beside me. The grip was talking: he didn't help George when I had his brother, it said, and now I couldn't interfere with this business. This business that must happen.

This was George's finest moment; he became a fully-fledged showman. He followed up his foot stamp with a vicious jabbing forefinger in Ali's left eyeball and when Ali doubled over, holding his weeping eye, with a final flourish,

George pushed him into the brambles at the clearing's edge. More perfect wrestling skills! And then the business was over. George had won and Ali offered no more resistance, rolling all cursing out of the thorns holding his wounded eye.

"George takes the chair," announced Blake, master of ceremonies, his voice tinged with a touch of brotherly pride.

Ali got up from the floor, his eye red and swollen.

"Don't cry," said Blake, looking Ali up and down with satisfaction. "Fourth in command now, eh?"

"You can stuff your gang," blurted out my friend, choking back tears. Blake puffed up, a bit shocked, not used to having his word challenged. And then I realised that Ali was looking straight at me, waiting for my support. The time we discussed by the canal had suddenly, too suddenly, arrived: we had to move to defeat the Dukes together now or we would be forever lost. But we had already lost. George had defeated Ali and that left Blake for me. And I had no chance there. Blake's still had my arm in his grip and I could only stare miserably at the floor.

"Piss off then mate," scoffed Blake. Had he waited to see if I held my silence? "Watch out though. We'll be looking out for you."

Ali looked at me one last time and, not being able to bear the hurt in his eyes, I ducked my head again. I heard Ali turn and slink away. Tears welled up inside me but my terror of the brothers and my need to survive won out and I kept my face straight. George threw a last stone in Ali's direction and Blake released my arm. The blood flowed again and I went all light, a flash of adrenalin. My heart boomed. Something from a wildlife television programme we had watched at school flashed through my mind: fight or flight? Fight or flight?

Blake flopped luxuriously into his armchair. "Sit down," he said, his voice all kindly now, gesturing towards the sofa that was suddenly for one person only. Ali's ejection from the gang had been so sudden and unexpected that despite the Dukes brothers acting all cool, I couldn't help but wonder if they were a little shocked themselves.

A long game of silence followed. For what seems like hours, no one spoke. Blake stared moodily into space, thinking maybe. George continued his idiot game of hit-the-can, occasionally rising from his new chair to get some more stones. I measured my breath, willing myself invisible as I waited for the order to go home that must come from our leader, the breaking of the spell. Silently, I tried to manage my emotions as I tried to look relaxed on the couch. Inside though, I was all beaten up by the animal attack on Ali. I was scared for my future in the new regime and full of guilt over the betrayal of my friend.

Time stretched, trickled, and finally disappeared entirely. Still no one spoke. I doubted I would manage a word ever again. The light faded until I could only just make out George's outline at the edge of the clearing. We never stayed so late the camp. Was Blake, doubting our ability to get home, just like me?

Blake suddenly shifted and there was a slim beam of light dancing before my eyes. No wonder he had been so cool, he had a torch with him all along.

"You did well today, Rich, at the tracks." The shock of his voice after the hours of silence was quickly absorbed into the blanket of dark and I smiled shyly at the unexpected praise, its warmth. Despite my anger and confusion, I felt a flood of relief, a strange desire to please Blake, to stay out of the path of his anger.

I tried to make out his expression, looking for mockery, to pick out sarcasm in his words, but I couldn't find any.

"Next time we go out at night."

My face was held in the sickly torch beam. I nodded weakly, stretching a smile. Blake swung the beam round the clearing to highlight George in his new chair.

"Up for a night attack, fatty?"

"Course." George grinned happily; no insult could darken his mood.

"Good." Blake switched the torch off and all was black. "We'll do it. Tomorrow night."

Business complete, Blake led us through the night, shining the torch in front of us. We picked our way through the outskirts of the dump and stumbled back towards the fuggy streetlight haze. We stopped at the corner of St Barnabas Close.

"Tomorrow," said Blake carefully, scanning my face under the yellow wash. "You get busy. We need bombs at the place. At least 20. 25. Tomorrow night we see you at the rec, eleven 'o' clock?"

"I think so..."

"You have to," he said quietly. George loomed behind him, still sneering.

I said nothing.

Blake nodded in satisfaction; he had me exactly where he wanted me.

"Good. See you then."

And they were gone.

Five
THE COME BACK KID

First thing, I was tapping gently on Ali's bedroom window. Ali lived on the first floor, in one of four rooms for rent on the first and second floors. His mum rented the one bedroom flat in the basement. I guess Ali's mum set up their home that way because it was cheap, she probably hated not having her son under her own roof, but at the time all I could see was my friend's independence, and I was pretty envious. He was like a grown-up, lodging up there with the print workers and students; and he could pretty much come and go as he pleased.

His face appeared at the window. No smiles. I tried a hopefully grin and he came to the door. In cream and red striped pyjamas and a black dressing gown, he looked like a boxer and I was reminded that since I had beaten George who had beaten Ali, I was currently ahead of him in the rankings. I wasn't fooled though: I knew Ali was my superior. All I wanted was to stop him hurting, to help him recover his dignity.

"What do you want?"

"Can I come in?"

He shrugged and I followed him into his room where he waved me into one of two chairs sitting before a small table by the window and sat down on his bed. Behind him there was a collage of Leeds United players, shouting out in agony and joy.

"What's Dukes saying?" I had never heard him call Blake by his surname. He might be a marked man, I realised, but he was actually free of Blake's control. I felt a brief pang of envy.

"Nothing. I mean he hasn't said anything about you..." I trailed off. Everything I said sounded like I was gloating.

Ali stared beyond me at the sun on the leaves of the oak tree outside his house. "I hate him."

I nodded sympathetically. In the collage behind Ali, Peter Lorimer took centre stage. I noticed for the first time that my friend had the same haircut, chocolate brown and shoulder length with a side parting beginning a couple of inches above his left ear and teased over his right eye. We stared at one another in frustration for a little while. Then Ali's mother broke the deadlock, knocking and coming in with two cups of tea and a plate of toast and jam. Seeing we had things on our minds, she put the food on the table and retreated. Ali took the chair opposite me, absently picking up a piece of toast as he sat down. I waited until I could hear his mother's footsteps on the staircase.

"How about we run away?"

"Right." Ali looked impatient. "Where to?"

"I don't know. Spain maybe."

"Spain?" Ali laughed, "Why Spain?"

"I've been before. It's cheap and sunny."

"And what would we do when we got there?"

"I went there after Dad died." At this point I needed to play the sympathy card. "There's a place there where people sleep on the beach. We could do that."

"OK, how are we going to get there? In a plane?"

"We could do. Or the train."

"Right. Who's going to pay for that then?"

I fell silent. Then something else occurred to me. "I know what we'll do." Ali looked up slowly, almost a sneer on his face. He had probably been thinking what an idiot I was to suggest we run off to Spain.

"What?"

"Something big. Prove ourselves to Blake, then leave the gang. Then they can't say we're chicken or anything."

Ali looked at me impatiently again. But he was listening. Encouraged, I continued.

"Blake wants to do a night attack tonight. He wants to meet me at the rec at 11. Then we're going to the place and we'll strike. You could come."

Ali looked away again. "No."

"You could be there. At the place, the nook... when we get there..."

His face brightened fractionally. I could tell he was tempted by the chance to redeem himself. "If I was there waiting it might spook him," Ali said slowly, "He might listen if we said we were finished afterwards. In the night."

"We'd have proved it."

We dunked our toast and jam into our tea, sucked up the sugary gooey mess and thought it through again.

Six

DS MACAULAY

So that night I waited for Blake and George, sitting on the foot of the kiddie's metal slide, getting my arse wet with dew, the zipper of my jacket up to my throat. Some distance away I caught the echo of some maniac laughing in the night. I shuddered. I was encased in the darkness of the rec, hemmed in the pen, the softness of the grass beneath my feet and the silence of the night ringing in my ears.

Time passed and the night gave me nothing. No Blake and no George. Maybe, I thought, I should run back to their house and shout their names out until they emerged to keep their promise. No, I realised grimly, that would not be a good idea. I simply needed to follow orders. And I had. I was where I should be. But there was Ali. He would be arriving at the nook alone soon, waiting with the 50 clay bombs we had made as a peace offering earlier that day. I needed to meet him. I owed him that.

Suddenly I froze. Someone was walking towards the fence at the side of the park. I tried to will myself invisible and measure my breath, but my heart was hammering against my rib cage.

I heard a high-powered torch click on and a slim, precise beam shot into the night. It searched the road towards the meadow efficiently and then turned and stopped precisely on me. I was blind, blinking and exposed, like a mole at the mercy of a marauding owl.

"What are you doing in there?" The voice was clipped and authoritative, confident but tinged with curiosity. I lifted my hand across the beam, shielding my eyes, squinting as I tried to make out the man behind the voice. The torch beam held me like tweezers.

"Nothing, I..."

"Nothing! Come on lad. What the hell are you doing in there?"

"I'm waiting for a friend," I said. I tried for an assured tone. "Leave me alone."

"A friend! Why would a boy like you meet a friend here, at this time of night?" This voice was impossible to resist. It invited confession, the relief of the unburdening of truth. "Come on, you're not safe in there are you?"

"It's about a girl."

"Bollocks. Get out here."

"No."

"Here. Now!" Parade ground stuff, military barking.

I clambered shakily to my feet, hoping now that the Dukes would come and supply a diversion; get me out of this mess. I didn't know who this voice belonged to, but I did know that its owner would do with me exactly as he wanted. I felt the power draining from my legs, my energy sapping.

The torch beam led me towards the gate, guided my fumbling hands as I pulled back the spring on the gate's bolt, and beckoned me towards it. Now I could see a squat wiry torso in a green puffer jacket. A muscular hand with black wiry hair on the back reached into an outside pocket, offering me a glimpse of garish orange lining, and returned holding a plastic wallet. The hand flipped the wallet open casually and I could see an ID card: a crest and a passport sized photograph of my interrogator, a man in his mid-thirties, fit and alert with a head of tight curls.

"Police. DS Macaulay, Thames Valley," he said, waving the

torch at his own face to confirm that it was his photograph on the card, "Now, you. What's your name?"

"Richard."

"Richard who?"

"Richard Turner."

"Richard Turner, I see. How old are you, Richard?"

There seemed little point in lying. "13."

"13? Do your parents know you're out, Richard?"

"No."

"No? Of course they don't. You're in trouble, Richard. What are you really doing here at this time of night?"

"I told you. I'm waiting for a friend. Really..."

"A friend? What friend?"

Ridiculously, it crossed my mind that the Dukes were listening, lurking in the shadows. I wouldn't implicate them: they would appreciate my loyalty. But Ali would understand why I had to give his name.

"Ali."

"Ali who?"

"Johnston. Alistair Johnston. He's 14."

"Well, where is he?"

"I don't know," I was feeling foolish. The quick fire questions were demoralising and I was worn out by their rapidity and impatience. Suddenly I felt very tired, ready for my bed, willing to do anything this man demanded.

"What time are you meeting him then? This Alistair Johnston."

"11 o'clock."

"11?" This time, the jeering voice annoyed me. Macaulay was parroting me, repeating each snippet of information I offered, mocking them and throwing my useless answers back at me, as if I was supposed to laugh at them too. Macaulay pulled up his sleeve, showing me a tough looking silver watch. "It's quarter to 12 now, Richard. I don't think Ali's coming. Do you?"

I shook my head miserably. A quarter to 12! Ali would be giving up at the nook, feeling angry and let down, all his efforts come to nothing. As for the Dukes, they were probably fast asleep in their beds: Blake had never intended to come. I realised he had played me for a fool from the start.

"What's your address, Richard?"

"15 Hart Close."

"15. Ali's?"

"He lives upstairs from his mum. Downstairs flat at 24 Walton Crescent." I could see the police cars arriving, the shock and disbelief on the faces of our mothers, the phone calls to school and the recriminations.

"See this?" Macaulay shone his torch inside his jacket again, this time revealing a handheld radio. "Everything you've said, they've heard down the station. It's all being checked now."

I was defeated. Now, like a helpless fish on the end of a line, all energy expended. I waited dumbly for Macaulay's next move. As if to underline my defeat I heard the distant scream of a northbound train in the distance, the last one. This was the train we were supposed to attack. Was Ali carrying out a lone assault? Somehow, even in the despair of my capture, I hoped so.

"Come on," said Macaulay grimly, "the car's this way."

I walked with the policeman over the bridge. He made no attempt to handcuff me or to steer me. But his supreme confidence, the power of his word, held me. And yet, as we walked into the light I felt more relaxed; I felt a bit like I was Macaulay's equal. I felt a strange affinity for his strength, for his assurance. We walked side by side to where he had parked a dark blue Hillman in the shadows. I took the passenger seat and he climbed in beside me. There was a strong smell of aftershave and cigarettes; on the dashboard, a packet of Players No10s and a paperback book, a war story. An imposing radio set was the only item that showed this was a plain-clothes policeman's vehicle. Otherwise the car could have belonged to anyone. Macaulay took a cigarette from the packet and hooked it into his mouth. He waved the packet in my direction and I realised with a slight shock that I was being offered one. That pleasing feeling of being Macaulay's equal returned. He wanted to smoke with me, I thought, to share a male ritual. I didn't smoke, never had, but I was tempted.

Then I realised he was testing me. I shook my head and thanked him politely.

"Good." Macaulay struck a match and lit up, took a deep drag and drawled his spent smoke into the night air. "You seem like a nice kid. From Hart Close you say?" His voice had softened up a bit as he smoked. He turned to look at me in the half dark.

"Yes."

"And who lives there with you?"

"My Mum. And I've got two sisters too."

"Dad?"

"My dad's dead, he died, he..."

"Dead?" He looked at me carefully then exhaled again. "I see," he said finally, flicking open an ashtray on the dash and tapping his ash into it. Inside there was a nest of crumpled orange butts. "How's your mum coping?"

"All right." I was puzzled by the questions. Where were they leading?

Outside the streets were deserted. Macaulay looked thoughtfully at the shadows then screwed his cigarette into the ashtray with an air of finality. "Well, look, it's probably best we don't worry mum with all this." He reached forward and turned off the radio and I nodded weakly and gratefully. I was to be released. "The best thing to do I think, is that I give you damn good hiding."

I was shocked. Was Macaulay saying he would beat me as a punishment for straying from my house at night, or was he suggesting a more formal punishment? Caning, rapped knuckles? Is this, I thought desperately, how justice is served out in the world of adults, of men? Yes. I was being asked to take my punishment like a man or I was not a man; or else I belonged to the blubbing world of women and children. Macaulay was opening a door to me and no matter how much feared it, I had no choice but to go through.

"All right." My voice was hollow.

"Good." Macaulay smiled, thrust his key into the ignition; the Hillman whirred into life and we took off.

We drove in silence. The streets were deserted and the big houses on Woodstock Road looked like crumbling castles. My stomach churned and my throat was stifled with fear; panic trapped in it like food. I breathed stiffly and carefully, as if I was a stowaway in Macauly's car and one ragged or uneven breath would expose me. He steered and shifted, full of confidence, piloting the purring Hillman north of the city. We glided through the streets in near silence. I dared to think about my punishment again. I had been promised a damn good hiding but Macaulay had not said where this hiding would be delivered. Perhaps we were heading for his house. I stared at the big detached houses and their lonely driveways. Perhaps we would turn into this one, or this, or this. I imagined the crunch of gravel under tyre, the soft thud of the doors closing and the wink of the welcoming carriage lights.

And then suddenly I saw the whole thing for what it was, a monstrosity. To agree to climb into this car with this man had been stupid. What I should have done, I could see clearly now, was to run. But where would I have run to? I pictured myself haring into the dark of the rec like a desperate animal, picked out by Macaulay's torch beam as I clawed hopelessly at the walls that bordered the football field. What would Blake have done? I tried to picture the gang leader in my situation but the image would not stick. I reached a dreadful truth: Blake would not have let this happen to him.

At the roundabout at the top of the Woodstock Road we took the first turning towards Wytham. We were heading back towards the meadow and now I could see that my punishment would take place not in a house but outside, on the meadow. Any hopes of a civilised occasion were disappearing fast; this would be barbaric. My hand tested my door handle lightly; I thought about flinging it open and pitching myself onto the grass verge. But I knew I had no choice: my destiny was cast. I had to accept all the pain and hurt that this man wanted to visit on me. This is what being a man was, I realised with perfect clarity, the capacity to absorb pain and not cry about it.

I glanced at Macaulay; he seemed vacant now, a man lost in thought. His eyes flicked and his toes prodded smoothly; he drove like a dancer, with rhythmic precision and steely confidence. He knew exactly what he was doing.

We crossed the north end of Port Meadow between the top of the city and the village of Wolvercote and lurched over a humpbacked bridge where the brick sides were close and most cars slowed down. Macaulay shot through at a steady clip, the bridge inches from his wing mirrors. I glimpsed the silent railway lines stretching into the night, a reminder of my stupidity.

Then, without warning, Macaulay squeezed the brakes and steered the Hillman into a car park adjacent to the meadow. He parked neatly in a far corner and hopped out purposefully.

"Come on," he called. His tone was cheerful and cajoling, like a games teacher encouraging a promising pupil to set a record at the high jump. I climbed uneasily out of the car. Macaulay pointed towards the dark of the meadow. "Walk," he said. He caught a glimpse of doubt on my face. "Just walk. Out there. I'll follow."

I opened a wooden gate and made out into the dark. I could barely hear him behind me. His boots made no noise as he trod carefully and deliberately on the grass but his corduroy trouser legs brushed against each other in a rhythmic swish, like windscreen wipers in the rain. This time he left his torch off: he did not want us to be seen. I could make out the edges of the meadow and the lights of the city in the distance but nothing else. Somewhere a horse blustered but I couldn't see it. I realised that if I were to cry out, no one but the horses would hear.

"Stop." Macaulay sounded tense, maybe even nervous. I could hear him breathing heavily. A ruffle of clothing. He had sat down. "OK here," he said. An order? An observation? A question? I was not sure but I thought about running again; I had a strong and clear impulse to fly. Fight or flight? Flight, flight.

"Come here."

Did he expect me to lie across his lap to receive a beating? He did. I realised I was to have my bottom spanked. Of course, I thought, like the naughty schoolboy I was. Ridiculous. Not sure what else to do, I moved awkwardly towards the policeman, unsure how to execute the movement required to sprawl across this man's lap in the dark. And then I could smell something in the air. Some half-remembered advice at school returned hard and real. Don't get in a car with strange men. Don't accept a lift from strangers. More. Playground shouts. Pervy pervert. Bag of sweets. Dirty old man.

I shuffled towards his outline. My mouth was dry. I began to speak but all that came out was a dry click in my throat. Fight or flight?

"Hurry up."

Flight.

Suddenly I was running, hard across the meadow in the night, in the dark. I could hear him cursing, stumbling to his feet but I was running faster than I ever had in my life. My trainers hit the ground like a drum roll, faster, faster. I heard his shouts. I was under arrest. He knew where I lived. He would be waiting. But I didn't break my stride. And I knew where I was heading too; Macaulay had brought me in a giant loop around the top of Oxford and I was not far from where I had been heading for earlier. I had a readymade bolthole where no one would find me: the nook.

I ran flat out for as long as I could, through a stitch and out the other side. My heart pounded, my chest burnt as I gasped for breath. Ahead of me was the grey outline of the copse, the way down to the tracks. I stopped, crouched down and my heartbeat and panting slowed. There were no footsteps behind me, no torch lights, no more shouting. I smiled wryly to myself; Macaulay couldn't keep up with me. In the distance I heard a car start up. The Hillman? Macaulay would be doubling back, hoping to cut me off as I came out from the meadow at the footbridge by the rec or further down parallel with my house. I felt an animal cunning inside me: I was a crafty fox with too much guile for the hounds. And the nook I would be safe, at least for the night. Then a wave of doubt. I considered the resources at Macaulay's disposal. He knew my address and, since I'd blurted it out, he knew Ali's too. He would be using that radio too. Soon the meadow would be crawling with police, searching for me. I was a criminal on the run.

Then a wave of confusion washed over me. What Macaulay had asked me to do was wrong. But somehow calling Macaulay a pervert, a child molester, seemed wrong too. The words conjured the peeping, energetic, frenetic character from the speeded up bit of the Benny Hill Show, a shiny, salivating man with greasy hair and a dirty raincoat. A pervert looked something like that: shiny and lithe, middle aged and polished. Macaulay seemed none of these things.

"Rich?"

I froze.

"Richard?"

"Ali?"

"Yeah. Where the hell have you been? I've been…"

"We need to get away. There's someone after me. We need to get back to the train throwing place."

"No trains now. Too late. I've been there for an hour, seen

three go through earlier but..." He stopped because I was staring at him hopelessly. "Where's Dukes?"

I told Ali we had to get out of sight, get back to the nook. I would explain it all when we got there. We picked our way back down to the tracks. Ali lit a torch but I told him to put it out, told him the police were looking for us. He swore softly. When we reached the nook, we crawled into the safety of the buddleia. Ali briefly lit his torch and we cleared a space on the earth floor. It was a warm night but I wished we had blankets or something to mark this out as a camp. I told Ali about the Dukes not showing, about Macaulay and about running away. He listened carefully. "I would have done what you did. You done the right thing."

"Do you think he was really a policeman?"

"I don't know. Policemen don't ... I don't know. How do you know he was? A policeman I mean."

"He had a card. And a proper radio. And he talked like a policeman. He..." I paused. How had he talked like a policeman exactly? "He could tell when I was lying." I said eventually.

"What are you going to do now?" I felt a chill run down my spine. Ali said had 'you' not 'we'. I was on my own.

"I don't know. Go to Spain." I smiled at my friend, looking for reassurance.

Nothing came back.

"Seriously, Richard."

"Well, I don't know. Maybe I should I give myself up."

"Maybe. Maybe..."

We lay back for a while, listening. The night was still, no cars, trains, birds. Nothing.

"We could go to my dad's," said Ali suddenly, "He'd know what to do."

"OK then."

"We'll know in the morning, we'll know what to do then."

"Ok then."

Seven

A BOY UNDERWATER

I woke up shivering and pulled my hands into the sleeves of my jacket, making fists to keep the cold air out. I took in the root-veined recess in the gathering half-light. The train throwing spot, the nook, our hideaway. Ali slept in front of me, pale in the gathering dawn. I lay there a while thinking about last night and imagined runaway lives on faraway beaches, waking under an upturned Spanish fishing boat, shaking sleep out off our bodies and preparing ourselves for ... for what? What would we do exactly? The alternative: Turning myself in at the police station. Could I accuse Macaulay of something? Fight back? Have my day in court? No. I wondered if I had been missed at home yet - Mum let me sleep in till about 10 o'clock sometimes so probably not – and I felt a burst of longing for the comfort of my warm bed at home. But that comfort was something I had known prior to last night and now only the nook was safe. No one knows we are here, I thought. Not mum, or Uncle Paul or the police. Except...Blake and George.

That realisation jolted me properly awake. I levered myself onto an elbow and looked out of the bush at the nook. The bombs Ali and I made to please Blake were sitting there, just in front of us, out of sight of the trains. I had forgotten about them. In the morning light they looked crude and dirty, like pieces of rubbish.

Then I felt a train coming, a vibration in the ground beneath our bodies, growing in intensity. I heard the tracks ping and rattle in expectation, heard the air rushing, the clatter of the wheels, the roar of the diesel and there it was again. Still magnificent. I watched Ali's eyes open as the rattle and rush subsided.

"Morning. Sleep well?"

"Not bad." He sat up and looked around him. "We've gotta go."

"Where?"

"Reading. My dad's. Unless you've got a better idea."

A mad grin spread across my face. We'll know in the morning, he had said, we'll know what to do then. And he did know: my magnificent mate. "How we going to get to Reading?" I asked.

"Walk. You can take the river path. It goes all the way. You got any money?"

"I can steal some."

"We'll do that."

We picked ourselves up and, on a whim, stashed the bombs out of sight. Then we set off back up the railway line, scrambled up the bank and emerged from the trees with the dewy green of the meadow spread out before us. The sun was spreading gold velvet behind us over the city and the air was filled with the cries of birds.

"It's called the dawn chorus," I said.

"What is?"

"The birds. I don't know why they sing in the morning though."

"Maybe they sing all the time. Maybe it's just quiet now."

We fell silent. Our plan was to go to my house, take all the money in mum's purse and head off to Reading. I didn't know what time it was but I guessed it was pretty early - there was still a nip in the air and not a soul in sight - and I should be able to let myself in, grab the money and go. We walked along the edge of a copse of poplars, trying to stay out of sight as much as possible as we made our way towards the road that would lead us back towards my house. We were on the lookout for police and trying to keep out of sight, so when we saw an elderly woman walking her dog in the distance, we ducked into the trees and waited for her to pass.

In amongst the poplars, we dropped down in the damp long grass. Its moisture was refreshing and I closed my eyes, I could have slept again. Maybe I did, just for a minute. But then Ali was tapping me hard on the shoulder. He pointed into the trees. I couldn't see what he was trying to draw my attention to at first but then I saw a battered leather boot. At first I thought it was a piece of abandoned rubbish. But then I saw it was attached to a leg and that another leg, clad in filthy navy corduroy like the first, was beside it with an identical scuffed boot at its end. Slowly, silently we rose to our feet and knew we are looking at Ned Shanklin, lying face down and spread in the grass as if he had plummeted there from the heavens.

Silently, gingerly, we circled the prone figure of Shanklin until we were standing either side of his clutch of dark curls. He lay stock still, his face obscured, either drunk, asleep or dead, we didn't know which. No sign of life, no even rise and fall of breath, his broad back lay still, lifeless. We looked at each other. Were we standing over a corpse? Should we've been calling the police? Or an ambulance? But I remembered then that the law were after us, we were fugitives. We had no choice but to leave the body. Then I noticed two more.

Mary Sullivan and Tim Physics were sprawled on their backs about 20 feet from Shanklin and about 30 feet from each other. Unlike Shanklin, they lay on their backs. A beam of morning sun had broken through the trees and bore directly down on Mary Sullivan's eyelids. Her neck and a shoulder were exposed too; like Shanklin, she lay as if she had fallen from a plane, sprawled like discarded meat in the grass; a tiny insect carelessly crawled up her chin.

Shanklin and Sullivan lay apart, opposite one another like

the hands of a clock showing a quarter past six. Physics was to be found at the clock's nine position. This time I had no doubt that I was looking at a corpse. Physics' eyes were closed, his features flat and placid.

At the center of this collection of the prone bodies, where their boots pointed, the remains of a fire smouldered, soft, grey ash still warm to the touch, surrounded by a gruesome collection of spent bottles. As one we turned to 12 o'clock, to the head of the ghastly body cross. We knew what we would find there, but we still gasped at the sight of the upright cowboy boots over the mess of Wild Bill's body lying face down next to a rotting log. Belle's mournful face turned towards us from where she lay beside her master, faithful to the last. "We should go," I mouthed. And Ali nodded.

We crossed the rail tracks via the bridge by the ironworks and walked purposefully past the factory gates. Workers were flooding onto shift, dressed in navy overalls, some smoking in silence, some calling out friendly greetings and good-natured jibes to one another.   Nothing unusual on Kingston Road either: just the woman at the bakers winding the canopy out in front of her shop window. No police cars in sight. Ali and I approached my house from the rear, via a rough, overgrown path where the bins were. The house looked serene, curtains drawn, early morning sun falling on the roof. It would have been easy to just let myself in and take to my bed, wait for the knock at the door and the arrest. But I remembered Ali had backed me when he didn't need to, supported his idiot friend in his hour of need. I told Ali to wait, scrambled over the gate and found the spare key under a stone.

The house was quiet, Rachel still sleeping. Good girl. In mum's handbag was a purse with £6.37 in change and, folded up small, five more pounds. I took the lot, stuffing it into my jeans pocket and then, on an impulse, opened up the fridge and looked for some food. I pulled out a lump of cheese and some cold sausages with hard lumps of white fat clinging onto them, added a jumbo box of matches and then, when I turned to see about grabbing some bread too, I saw Rachel staring up at me from the doorway.

She was looking mischievously up at me, a dummy hanging out of the corner of her mouth and a sagging nappy behind her.

"Reech."

"Rachel, what are you doing out of bed?"

"Wanna be sick."

She didn't look as if she wanted to be sick. She took the dummy out, threw it on the floor and threw her gummy mouth open wide. She wanted to play. Upstairs all was quiet. I looked down at my jeans and jumper: they were covered in mud and dust.

"Wanna be sick."

"Rich?" Mum's voice from the top of the stairs. Now: go or be captured.

Run out the door.

Go.

Or.

Be sick. In the cupboard were biscuits. Biscuit. Be sick.

"Rich? Is Rachel with you?"

I tried to keep my voice calm as I called up the stairs, "Yes mum, she wants a biscuit."

"Give her a rusk. I'll be down in a minute."

"OK mum. Mum?"

"Yes."

"I've got to go out. I'll see you later mum."

She called something back but I didn't hear. I was mumbling something to myself, saying goodbye.

I shook myself focused again, gave Rachel a biscuit and sat her on the sofa. I turned on the TV and she was gone, lost in the colours and the music, instantly captivated as she slobbered on the rusk. I put the sausages and the cheese in my school bag. Grabbed a toothbrush and a jumper from upstairs and I was gone.

Ali's house was easier. We just let ourselves in via his separate front door and went to work. We were a combined force, a winning team. We washed our faces in Ali's sink and emptied his piggy bank into his school bag. He chucked in a jumper and a toothbrush too. We stared, as if for the last time, at his Leeds collage. And he took his scarves, the silk one and the wool one.

We walked through the maze of Jericho's little terraced streets, crossed the canal at the footbridge near the boatyard and followed the canal path until we got to the sky blue railway bridge. Boat people, long haired hippies, were throwing open the little doors at the front of their barges and lighting their first roll ups of the day. We ignored each other. The heat was starting up again: another hot day on the way. I started up an adventure song. *Walking on the beaches looking at the peaches.* We added the bass and guitar parts, enjoying ourselves, the horrors of last night momentarily forgotten. Passing a canal boat we saw some bamboo poles stacked against a homemade bike shed and helped ourselves to one each.

We skirted the edge of the city, glorious and terrible outcasts. My mood roller-coastered: sometimes my spirits soared with the joy of freedom; sometimes a churning fear rumbled through my guts which threatened to destroy me. And sometimes I forgot we had run away entirely, that we were wanted by the police, that we had seen dead bodies this morning.

"Blake and George chickened out," I announced.

"Wankers."

I giggled at the image. "Whatever happens, they can't take away the fact that we were there. Ready to attack. We were there."

"They won't know I was there," said Ali, a bit sad suddenly.

"Well, I'll tell them," I shouted. "They won't boss us about anymore." To emphasise my point I beheaded some cow parsley with my bamboo pole. "Those tramps," I said, my bravado suddenly running out, "were they actually dead? All of them?"

"Yes. Shanklin wasn't breathing. I stood over him and watched his back. No breath. Nothing." Ali looked spooked too. We paused to watch a canal boat chug slowly up the canal towards the Isis lock.

"I dunno," I said, "when my sister and I were little we used to share a bedroom. Sometimes her snoring would wake me up and I'd lie awake listening to it. Then sometimes she'd go all still, not breathing for minutes, ages. Then just when I thought she'd definitely died, she'd start up snoring again."

Ali smiled. "My dad did that once. When we were camping."

"I don't know about Shanklin," I said, "but Tim Physics, he was definitely dead."

"I think his eyes were open."

I was pretty sure this was not true but I didn't want to disagree with my friend; I needed his loyalty too much. "In the sun," I added darkly.

We both shuddered. We had began to enjoy the revulsion a little.

"You think they've found them yet?" said Ali.

"Probably not. They were out of sight. In the long grass. No one will be looking for them. It will be the smell, dead body smell, that'll make anyone find them."

"Are we guilty? Of not telling?"

"I don't know," I said. Then I saw Blake and George ahead. They were sitting on a beam of the lock gate nearest to us. I could see that both gates were closed. Opening and closing the lock gates is something we did many times as a gang. We called it gating, operating the lock gates for the boats in exchange for tips. The lock connected the canal with the Thames and there was steady traffic moving to and from the river towards the boatyard. Sometimes the bargemen and often the tourists who hire the barges from the boatyard were happy to let us open the gates for them. Then we'd ask for a quid: the boatmen gave us 20 pence or told us to naff off, the tourists often paid up. Seeing Blake and George there, I forgot for a second all that had happened.

But then we saw them see us and get to their feet, their faces set hard. I wondered what had brought them here, so early, to the city limits, like ugly mutt gatekeepers baring our way. But it was too late to consider much, we were soon upon them.

"Look who it isn't," said Blake. All the bravery of a few minutes before seemed hopeless now. He looked at Ali, then at me. "Think you're too good for us now then?" he said.

"No." My voice was shaky.

"Why you with him then?"

Behind Blake, George leant over to spit carefully onto the path, then turned his dead eyes back on us.

"He's my friend," I began, "And we wanted to show you..."

Blake smiled at my weakness. We wanted to please him. He pressed home his advantage.

"Where were you last night anyway?"

My hopeless defence. "I didn't see you..."

"Bollocks."

"Chicken." George, brave and getting braver. I looked down at their docs, laced tight shut, ready to attack our ribs and skulls. Ali stayed quiet.

"No..."

"We waited half the night for you," said Blake casually, sitting down on the beam again. George remained on his feet, staring steadily at me.

"No. Look, I went. I waited at the rec. In the dark."

"In the dark?" Blake raised his eyebrows, laughing. "Were you frightened? In the dark?" George began to snigger. I felt irritation rising despite my fear of Blake. Leave me alone with George, I thought, just for a minute... "'Cos I reckon you're bullshitting," Blake continued, "'Cos me and George was really there. Weren't we George?"

George nodded, a stupid goofy grin on his face. The anger rose inside me. I couldn't tolerate him taking me for an idiot. I wanted to launch myself at him, maul him, destroy him.

"I was there," I shouted defiantly, surprising myself, "I waited for you and you didn't come. I got arrested."

"Arrested?" said Blake. His manner changed. His shoulders fell into a crouch, as if he was going to duck out of sight. He looked carefully around him before he spoke. "Who arrested you?" he said exactly.

"The police."

"You got picked up by the coppers?" Blake looked around again, scanning the towpath. But there was no one about; it was still early.

"Yeah. Just one. He..."

"Did you get done?" I realised with a bit of shock that Blake looked ruffled, as uncomfortable as I had ever seen him.

"No. Well, he said he'd beat me." My words, my story, sounded ridiculous even to me but I continued with it. "I ran off."

"You ran off? From the coppers?" I had to admit that a bit of me wanted to see him impressed. After all I'd defied the highest authorities, the police, the law. I wanted to see Blake's respect for that, see him look up to us for a change. Instead, Blake looked unsettled, almost embarrassed. He recovered his aggression quickly though and moved closer to me, face inches from mine. "Did you grass us up?"

"No! I wouldn't do that."

He was thinking; I could see he didn't know what to do. George had withdrawn to perch on the lock beam; he stared vacantly at the mid-distance in front of him, awaiting instructions. Blake looked at Ali.

"Was he there?" He cleared his throat. "Were you there?"

"No," said Ali carefully, "Not then. But I met him afterwards. We slept at the place last night, the nook, the train throwing place..."

"What were you doing out?" You could sense Blake's rising irritation. It was all too complex for him.

"We were going to surprise you," said Ali, "I was going to see you at the nook. I wanted to get back in the gang. We made 50 bombs. For you. For the gang."

Blake nodded, apparently satisfied for the moment by the display of loyalty. He turned to me again.

"What did you tell him? The copper."

"Nothing."

Blake nodded carefully then released a taut grin. "Good. Good for you." George grinned too, aping his elder brother. Blake appeared more relaxed. He looked carefully around him once more. Then suddenly he set his features hard again. "Bullshitters," he muttered, then shouting, "Get him, George!"

I saw Blake lunge at Ali, throw a punch; Ali caught Blake's arm but the momentum made him lose his footing; he stumbled to the floor, dragging Blake with him. George, greasy head low, charged me, hoping to knock the wind out of me. But I was ready for him. A clean uppercut on his cheek, crisp contact, the bone jarred and I felt his flesh tear and weaken. Still his lunge was in motion and his bulk bowled me to the ground beneath him. As I fell I saw Ali and Blake on their feet. I saw Ali land a punch on Blake. Small stones jarred my spine but now I knew we could win. No song arrived yet. Instead I was screaming in pain: George was biting me in the stomach. I grabbed his head and twisted it upwards. The skin on my belly ripped. Agony. I smashed him in the face as hard as I could; his jaw dropped like he'd been clapped on the back, releasing me from his bite. Punch drunk, out of it. I scrambled to my knees and took in the other battle. Ali was winning! Blake limply held his hands over his face, protecting himself from Ali's careful, measured blows. As I watched, Ali landed a choice strike on Blake's cheekbone. We were defeating the Dukes! The song arrived then: *We are the champions.* I straddled George and rained punches down on his doughy face, really let him have it. He was slobbering and whimpering but I couldn't stop. Everything was flowing through my fists: George was the meadow, Macaulay, the dead tramps, my dad, Tim Physics, Shanklin, Wild Bill, but most of all, he was Blake, he was Blake.

"Stop!" Blake was whimpering at Ali, backed against the side of the lock. He had stopped fighting back. His face was streaked with blood and his ear was cut. His hands were no longer balled into fists but held over his face like a mask. Here was where the mighty fell.

"Go on Ali," I hollered, "Go on! Kill him!"

Ali stepped back and landed a giant sucker punch on Blake's temple. Blake staggered backwards and then he was gone. A tremendous splash. He was in the lock.

For a moment all was silent. The path remained deserted. George twisted beneath me. Ali was frozen, his fists by his side. George was shouting something. I staggered to my feet. No sign of Blake. No sound. An urgent flurry of bubbles fizzled at the surface and then all was still.

"He can't swim!"

George was scrambling to his feet. All of us at the side of the lock. It was full. The water came up to about a foot from the top. No sign of Blake. I kicked off my shoes. I will save him, I thought, even though he might attack me in the depths, I will try to save him. My heart was leaping about like a dog. Real death, real murder. The tramps were nothing. Real murder.

The water folded around me, ice cold, greasy; I could feel the filth, the matter floating in it. I spat out the water from my mouth and forced my eyes open. I could see nothing, just murky dark, river weed maybe, no Blake. I stretched my arms and my legs out, feeling in the dark for his body. An explosion: Ali landed beside me. At first, I could barely see him through the dirty haze but then I could make out his hair, a swaying ghost. I saw his arms sweeping the water around him, looking for our enemy. We swept the water. Nothing. I flipped and dipped to the bottom of the lock and touched the slimy concrete floor. I looked around again. Nothing. My lungs were burning, head whistling.

I broke the surface. George was staring at me. His face swollen and bruised, he looked grotesque, like a cheap rubber toy.

"He can't swim!" he screamed at me again.

Ali surfaced too, panic in his eyes.

"You see him?"

He shook his head and dived again, deep this time. I followed. The same fruitless paddling and probing. Blake had disappeared.

When we both came up again, George was gone too. We swam to the side. We could see his squat form running away.

"George!" I shouted, hauling myself out of the water, "George!"

He stopped. He turned and looked beyond us to check we didn't have Blake then carried on.

We pulled ourselves out of the water and stood stunned and dripping. We were both quivering, neither of us knew whether it was through cold or through fear. Then the convulsions began. Rooted on the spot, teeth chattering, dripping relentlessly onto the mud where minutes before the Dukes' boots had stood. In the lock, all was still.

"We have to go," I said.

Ali nodded. We ran in the opposite direction from George. Away from the meadow, away from the city, away from home.

Eight

THE SITE

When I awoke, wild grass was scratching my face. I shifted my head back onto the wool of my jumper pillow. It was slightly damp with morning dew but wasn't unpleasant. I realised my body was warm because it was pressed against Ali's and felt a flush of embarrassment: we must have looked a bit odd, all cuddled up together like that. A rod of morning sun broke through the tree canopy above us and settled on my shoulder. I let the heat warm my bones and listened to a bird calling from the water. A Canada goose? Canada geese. Canada geese. Then a flurry of churning water as the bird spread its wings and took off, trailing its feet in the river. In the distance, I could make out the beat of a train too. Canada geese. Canada geese.

A ladybird crawled over my finger and I raised my chin from the ground to take a closer look at it. A fairytale shell: a comic book red cape with flamboyant spots. I turned my hand slowly to bring its head into view and blinked at the sight, a horrific Darth Vader mask, grotesque teeth, merciless eyes. Disgusted, I flicked the alien creature away. It landed on Ali's ear, settling on his lobe like a garish ear-stud. For a moment I was reminded of the horror of the dead tramps, their corpses laid out in the sun for the insects to pick over. Then that nightmare vision was replaced by another: Blake's body settling on the floor of the lock basin, eyes staring hopelessly towards the surface. A wave of repulsion and guilt washed over me. We couldn't find him but the police surely would. Or they already had. Now I imagined them hauling his dripping carcass out of the depths, George standing glumly to one side. The police - Macaulay there too - stand gravely in attendance as the limp form of our former leader is winched out before them. They ask George and he points downriver. It was them. Us.

Ali stirred. He shook the ladybird out of his hair, bucked his knees against mine, groaned and rolled onto his back. "What time is it?"

I looked at my watch. It had stopped at twenty to nine. Last night, yesterday morning or now? Then I saw. It wasn't waterproof: it marked the time of death. "Don't know. Early I think."

"What day?"

I had to think this one through. It was Thursday night when I sneaked out, Friday when we woke up in the nook, still early when Ali pitched Blake into the lock. It was Saturday. I told him so.

Ali lurched dizzily to his feet. I joined him, blinking at the trees and the fields around us. "Stig of the dump," he smiled, looking me up and down.

"Smelly boy." I smiled back, outlaws together again. "What we need," I said, "is food and a wash." The bread, cheese and sausages had got scoffed when we camped down the previous night. Now hunger was gnawing at our insides.

"We'll get washed in the river," said Ali. "Food we can steal or... we've got how much?"

I started to tot up our pooled funds and gave up. "We've got some."

"Starving."

I didn't answer. We had to keep moving. We were still less than ten miles from the scene of the crime but our distance from the offence was not really the point. I knew, we both knew, we couldn't escape, not really. Ali had murdered Blake, or at least was guilty of killing him accidentally, and I was an accessory. Sooner or later, we would be arrested, tried in a court of law, made to pay. We knew all this but thinking about the reality of it was unbearable, so we didn't. I stole a glance at my friend; God only knew what the hell was going on inside his head. Facing jail surely, the end of his young life. But if he was thinking of it, I could see no sign as he got to his feet and pushed his things into his rucksack.

We left the meadow and the oaks behind us and climbed over a wooden fence onto the edge of a field of rape. The yellow was luminescent and we instinctively reached for the golden flowers and crushed them in our hands as if we could transfer their energy to ourselves. In the east the sun was rising, bathing the field in a golden sheen. We shared a look, acknowledging the magic.

And then there was the authority of the muscular river. We emerged at its side on a rough mud path between the rape field fence and the riverbank. No sign of people, just Father Thames winding his way south. No boats; no walkers. We stripped down to our pants at the side of the river and were about to stash our bags in a ditch on the rape field side of the path when I remembered the dirty clothes, the state of us.

"We need to wash our clothes too," I said. "We've got to look clean. And...as well..."

"They're evidence," said Ali flatly. He was thinking the same way I was. I knew it then.

We returned to the bags and pulled out lumps of filthy clothes. Then we stepped in with our clothes held out before us, letting the soft mud ooze between our toes as we braced ourselves for the water's cold. But we only shivered briefly and soon we were paddling and stumbling into the river's mainstream where we could feel the water flow through the jeans, T-shirts and socks in our hands. We let the river wash away the dirt of yesterday and, laughing, refreshed and exhilarated, returned to the bank to lay our sopping clothes in the sun to dry, out of sight of the path, back in the golden rape field. And then we returned to the water to paddle on our backs, enjoying the sun as we kicked the river in arcs over our heads. It was going to be hot again. The charge of summer heat would change us, made us more wild, more free.

Then a boat. Ali heard it first. The thrum of an outboard motor approaching. We both smelt the danger straight away. This was no cabin cruiser. Its tone was urgent, insistent: the snarl and roar of a hunter. Chest deep in the water, we stared in panic at one another, exposed.

"Get out," shouted Ali.

"No time," I muttered. I tried not to panic but the engine's gnawing buzz was close, perhaps round the next bend. We scrambled towards the bank but there was no cover there: some rushes, wild long grass, the exposed path. Upriver, in the direction of the noise, I glimpsed a mast, moving fast with animal cunning, a radio antennae. I knew it was the police. And then I knew what to do.

"Breathe in," I said, calm now, like a family doctor issuing a routine instruction. "Deep breath."

I watched Ali obediently inflate his chest and puff his checks and I did the same. We held our noses and Ali knew what I was thinking then: as one we ducked beneath the surface.

Cold underwater silence again. A horrific reminder of Blake's watery grave. But now our thoughts were on our own survival. We reached down for the weeds on the riverbed to anchor ourselves to the floor. So much weed and dirt in the water, it teemed before our eyes as we opened them, clinging fast to the riverbed, locked out of sight. And we could hear the engine, echoing through the watery silence, see the water gush, gather and drag before us as the boat's propellers churned the river's guts. We saw the body of the boat, not two metres in front of us threatening to pull us apart. It pulled at us, threatening to upend us, to send us bobbing to the surface and deliver us to our captors.

A rising aching pressure in the lungs, a scream for oxygen. Hold on. I wedged my fingers under a large flat stone. The propeller, spinning in the gloom, sent bubbles across our faces and tugged at us again, stronger this time. I looked at Ali. He looked at me. We knew we were going to make it.

More pressure, water shoving at our limbs. We shook but held on, waiting for the water to calm. I felt a whistle in my head like a kettle boiling. No more good air in my lungs, only dead air, spent air. I must stand up now, I told myself dreamily. I looked to Ali again and saw his pants, side on. I realised this meant he had stood up but I couldn't join him. I could feel a glorious warmth. The water was welcoming me...

Ali grabbed me by the armpits and pulled me roughly to my feet. My lungs were burning. I breathed in deep. Water ran down my body. The boat had gone. Back to life. I felt the blood rush to my head, my vision cleared as if someone had run a windscreen wiper over it, and I realised I had nearly gone. But I knew then we could survive; knew we had it in us.

We understood what had just taken place - how close we were to joining Blake – but we didn't talk about it. We didn't need to. We returned to our clothes, already nearly dry in the heat, and sat in the sun for a while, drinking in its energy. Then we took off through the rape again and hit a half path out of sight of the river that skirted the field and bordered a copse with the railway line on the other side. Back with the rhythm of trains in our earshot - Canada geese Canada geese - we headed south once more.

We walked all morning, staying on the rough path running parallel to the tracks, separated from it by a bed of nettles and a wire fence. To our left a village loomed and we turned away from the tracks and headed towards its centre. We saw the first people we had seen since we'd killed Blake, a middle-aged couple with a dog, and smiled because they didn't look twice at us. We had done a good job at the river: bodies washed and our clothes clean and sun dried; we looked like two normal kids.

We found a village shop nestled in ivy and we bought a loaf of sliced white bread, ham in a flat plastic pack and two Mars bars. The lady behind the counter didn't give us a second look either. We felt the power of invisibility as we handed over some of our funds and then, salivating with hunger, headed for a corner of the village green to stuff our gobs. We stashed the remainder of the food into my pack and drank our fill from a tap outside the shop and then headed back towards the river down a meandering country lane. Seeing a footpath leading off the tarmac, we took it and soon found ourselves in the cool of a wood.

I remember that wood like something out of a fairy tale: rays of pure sunshine dropping through a leafy canopy high above our heads like spotlights onto a stage. Saplings reached for the light and dead trees rotted where they had fallen, blending into the mossy carpet of bark remains beneath our feet. We were following a rough path with bracken on either side when Ali stopped.

"I think someone threw something."

I stopped too then and we scanned the silent wood. It mocked our vigilance. Somewhere far away a wood pigeon cooed us softly back to the nook.

"You sure?"

"I think something hit my back."

We looked around again and seeing nothing still, shrugged and walked on.

Then I felt a sharp tap on the crown of my head. A small stone. No doubt.

"I've been hit too."

We stopped dead and looked carefully around us. Silence again. Then a scuffle in the bracken. I saw a flurry of movement, scrambling limbs, a flash of fur.

"What the...? You see that?"

"What was it?"

"Dunno..."

Another stone hit me hard on the cheek. The missiles were coming from ahead of us; someone was throwing stones at us from the bracken at the edge of the path ahead.

"Hello?" shouted Ali. No reply.

"Who are you?" I pitched in.

This time a stifled laugh. Kids?

Ali came to the same conclusion as me and we charged the bracken. As we reached the edge of the path, a kid took off. A longhaired little Herbert, no more than seven years old, but fast, sure of the woods. Ali and I were fast too though and longer legged and we gained on him quick. Soon he was in grabbing distance and I reached out and got hold of a shoulder. A filthy face, streaked with mud and eyes alive with fear, looked back at me and he ducked out of my grip. Then, as he headed away from my grasp, he tripped over a root and fell headlong into a patch of brambles. He screamed as the thorns cut his face and I stopped, unsure of how to pull him out, and whether I should at all.

Ali arrived and took charge, hoisting the kid out by the scruff of his neck and his filthy jean waistband, lifting him bodily clear of the bramble bush. A scruffy boy, hair cropped on top and long at the back, a dirty, furtive little face streaked with tear tracks looked defiantly up at us; he knew we didn't know what to do with him. Ali held his shoulders tight and crouched down in front of him. I stood behind Ali, trying to look tough.

"What do you think you're doing?" said Ali, "Throwing stones at us?"

The kid looked sulkily at the floor, then looked up, brave, leering at us. He knew we didn't have it in us to hit him. Then he brightened, started grinning wickedly. His eyes were looking beyond Ali and beyond me. We turned around. Another bigger kid was standing in front of us, a girl about our age, with a cold hard stare and a gleaming switchblade in her hand. My legs turned to jelly and my arms dropped passively to my side.

"You'll leave my brother alone," said the knife girl, a thick country accent tinged with an Irish lilt. We realised we were looking at a proper tough, around our age maybe, but a different breed: combat trousers, steel toecaps and a mop of black curls framing sharp features and merciless green eyes. Chunky gold earrings glinting, she held the knife confidently, in front of her like a water diviner, loose and relaxed, ready to strike.

Ali took his hands carefully off the kid's shoulders and, keeping his hands raised and clear of his body in open palmed surrender, turned towards the girl. The urchin skipped round us to stand next to his sister and grin viciously at our plight.

"Who are ya?" drawled the knife girl.

"No one," said Ali.

"No one?"

"We're criminals," I blurted, "On the run..."

Ali nudged me quiet. Knife girl smirked as she looked us incredulously up and down. "The hell you are," she said finally.

"It's true. We're murderers. The police are looking for us."

"Rich, shut up."

"Who ya murdered then?" asked the girl. We had at least piqued her curiosity.

"A kid," I said, "He tangled with us so...." I shrugged and tried as hard as I could to look like an unrepentant hardcore killer.

"How d'ya kill 'im?"

"Drowned him. With my bare hands."

The knife girl nodded slowly. Somehow I had managed to impress her or at least earn a stay of execution. She let the knife fall slowly to her side and then folded it away with an air of finality.

"My name's Brenna," she said. "This here is Squirrel." She shoved her brother towards us. "He's sorry he threw stones at ya." Squirrel looked anything but sorry, staring hard and silent at us. "He don't talk," she added.

"Rich," I said, holding out a hand. I pointed at Ali. "That's Ali."

She ignored my hand. "Where you from?"

"Nottingham." Somehow I imagined this would sound a more suitable hometown for an outlaw on the run than plummy Oxford.

"Nottingham? Where's that then?"

"Up north."

"You walk all the way here then? From up north?"

"Yeah," I grinned. "Feet are killing us."

Brenna smiled too. "C'mon," she said and turns on her heel. We followed her into the woods and tramped through long grass until we reached a clearing. The charred remains of a fire formed a centre point with logs dragged around it for seats. Brenna waved at us to sit down.

"Ask Arthur for two bowls of stew," she told Squirrel. "Bring 'em back here." Squirrel shook his head emphatically. "I know. 'Ee'll say, you've already 'ad yer share but let 'im know I need 'em. Tell 'im I'm starving." She rubbed her tummy enthusiastically, opened her mouth wide and rolled her eyes. "Tell 'im..." Brenna paused to consider the resources at her disposal. "I'll definitely bring 'im up a rabbit later," she said at last, "maybe two."

Squirrel continued to look doubtful but Brenna hissed and shooed him out. Squirrel turned and bolted for the edge of the clearing; he disappeared out of sight where the ground dropped away at the clearing's edge.

"Thanks," I said. It didn't seem right to tell this wild young woman that we had just eaten.

Brenna nodded and pulled out a pouch of rolling tobacco, freed an individual leaf from a clump of tangled cigarette papers, sprinkled it with tobacco and then carefully folded the packet before waving it in our direction. We shook our heads and Brenna looked hard at us after that. Proper criminals should be smoking, she was thinking. She glanced at our jeans and T-shirts then and sized up our schoolboy faces. We looked like what we were, ordinary kids out of our depth, no doubt. I decided it was about time I changed the conversation.

"How come he don't talk?" I said, pointing at Squirrel.

"How come he don't talk?" she countered, pointing at Ali.

"I do," said Ali indignantly and raised a laugh out of Brenna.

"Couldn't tell ya why Squizz don't talk," she said lightly. "He just don't. Never has. He ain't stupid, mind."

I nodded. "Where do you live?"

Brenna looked carefully at me, as if she was sizing up the extent of our trustworthiness. Then she waved a hand airily in the direction Squirrel had headed off in. "Got a site. Just down there. Twenty-three vehicles."

"Vehicles?"

"Yeah, vehicles. Trucks. Vans." We must have been gawping at her in incomprehension because she stabbed out the next phrase as if addressing idiots. "My family. We live on the road." Then, after smartly sparking her rollup cigarette with a battered metal lighter, she got up and motioned for us to follow. At the edge of the clearing where the land dropped away, the direction Squirrel had darted off, we could see through the trees open country spread out to the south, the crest of the Ridgeway in the distance, the giant cooling towers at Didcot and, directly below us, the roofs of caravans and large vans, with canvas canopies and brightly coloured blankets forming tents between them. At the centre of the camp we could see a large fireplace and a towering pile of logs and big branches. A few unkempt figures, burly men and one woman, sat smoking by the unlit fire enjoying the sun on their faces. We watched the tiny figure of Squirrel run towards the group and point in our direction. They looked up but couldn't see us through the trees. We heard them laugh at Squirrel's urgent gestures and presently a large man with tattoos and a long ponytail got to his feet and headed towards a coach. He disappeared inside and came back with an earthenware pot that he handed to Squirrel who then set off back towards us.

"How long you lived here?" I asked Brenna, trying not to sound too impressed.

"Not long. Few weeks maybe. Old Bill'll move us on soon probably but we don't care. Plenty of places to go."

"How old are you?"

"Full of questions, ain't ya?" I looked at the softness of her cheeks and quickly took in the beginnings of breasts under her shirt and guessed that she might be our age or thereabouts. But her behaviour was one of a much older person, coarser and wiser than someone of our age could be.

"Do you go to school?"

Brenna laughed but not, I thought, because my question was ridiculous. "No. I don't go to school."

"Too old?"

"No. I'm school age. But I don't go."

"What?" My mouth fell open in a dopey smile as I took in what she was saying. Here was a world where people roamed the world in beaten up old vans without a care in the world and children didn't have to go to school.

"Never been," she said proudly, "Well, I did go once actually. When I was six, Avebury way."

"What happened?" I asked.

"It was shit so I left." We all laughed, Ali joining in too. "My dad," she continued, "Arthur, bloke you seen just then who give Squizz the stew, he told the bloke from the council who come up the site, my girl don't have to go 'cos she takes care of my son. Bloke said I had to, started waffling on about Arthur's legal responsibility and all that bollocks. Arthur told him to naff right off." We laughed again. "And 'ere's yer grub," said Brenna as Squirrel arrived with the earthenware pot, two bowls upside down as a lid. I saw that Brenna was a performer and enjoyed impressing us. I didn't know why, maybe she was buying the murderer line, maybe not, but I wasn't going to complain. We were sorely in need of a bit of help. Brenna poured a generous helping of vegetables and lentils into the bowls and handed them to us. We looked at the steaming bowls curiously, wondering where the spoons would come from, until she motioned to us to put the bowls to our lips and drink. When we did, we found it was delicious and slurped back the hot salty liquid and vegetables with gusto, our reluctance to eat forgotten. We felt comfortable then, enjoying the role of outlaws sating a hard won appetite. I remembered Will Scarlet chancing upon Robin Hood and his band of brigands and wondered if that was where Nottingham had came from. Brenna lit another fag and watched us eat while she smoked. When we finished, we gratefully put the bowls down and she looked at us squarely.

"Tell us about this murder then."

I looked at Ali. He shrugged. The way I saw it, the tough guy act wasn't going to work with this girl. She had already rumbled us, realised we were just a couple of kids on the run, out of our depth. Luckily, I thought, she seemed to like us, or liked me anyway. We might as well have told her the truth.

"We had a gang," I began, "but Blake, the leader, gave us a hard time. We had a fight and, well, Ali pushed him in the canal and he couldn't swim so... he drowned."

"With your bare hands?" mocked Brenna, and I shrugged, but there was a dance of laughter in her eyes. Then she looked at Ali coolly. "Still," she said slowly," you're in deep shit ain't ya? 'Specially you, killer. What you going to do?"

"We thought we'd go to his dad's," I said.

"Where's he then?"

"Southampton," I lied.

"We might go to Spain," said Ali, "or America maybe." I stole an incredulous sidelong glance at my friend. It was the first time I had heard mention of that.

"Oh it speaks!" exclaimed Brenna, her eyes lighting up. She turned to my friend. "America you say? You've got money then?"

"No. Not really but we'd walk there and work for the money or whatever..." Ali said quietly.

"Walk to America!" shouted Brenna and Squirrel laughed hard too this time, a curious silent shake. "You're effing mad you are!" Suddenly her face clouded. "You got Old Bill after you?" she asked darkly. We sat in stunned silence at the interrogative stare she was training on us. Squirrel's grubby face turned hostile again, the vicious grin returned.

"I dunno," I said at last. I remembered the police boat and the near escape. There was little doubt that they were. "They might be looking for us," I admitted.

"If you killed some kid, they'll be looking all right," said Brenna. She stubbed her cigarette out on the log beside her and looked at us carefully again. "Look. You're not fooling me. I can see you're wet behind the ears. Got yourself in deep with something you can't handle you have." She regarded us wearily, eyes boring into our faces, while Squirrel mimicked her scrutin. We could only nod meekly. "Did you kill a kid really?"

"Yes, we did," said Ali. Then, after thinking for a moment: "I did."

She nodded slowly again. "Deep deep shit you're in. You'll have Old Bill crawling everywhere looking for ya. The family, my dad and the others, they won't touch ya. They get enough shit from the law as it is, don't wanna coupla underage killer kids hanging about the site. You," she said a touch of pride creeping in to her tone, "are at our mercy." Squirrel nodded with satisfaction; she was right when she said he was not stupid, he was following every word.

"Well, we're not actually," said Ali suddenly, surprising us all. "We're grateful for the stew and everything but we should be on our way. My dad'll know what to do, whether to turn ourselves in or whatever. We actually don't need you at all."

Brenna laughed. Her mood towards Ali brightened immeasurably. "Fair dos," she said, "but I'll show you what I've got anyway. You can take it if you like, not if you don't and fair enough either way." She leapt up again and led us off into the woods in a direction we hadn't been in before, onto a tiny path through some dense brambles that reminded me of the way into our camp back at the dump. Then we headed off that path, ducked under more brambles and emerged in a clearing where a crude igloo shaped shelter had been fashioned out of sticks and branches. Brenna stood proudly to one side as I took a look inside. There was a floor of soft dry bark and a couple of blankets laid out, some candlesticks and matches on a large flat stone. It was a perfect hideaway.

"Stay here tonight if you want," said Brenna, "And you can come down the site later. We've got a party on. They'll all be blind drunk, won't notice you. We'll have a cider or two and then, in the morning..." She cocked a thumb over her shoulder.

In the morning we would go. We nodded in understanding.

"Anyway, take it easy, sleep if you want," said Brenna smiling and pointed at the camp. "Come dusk time, me and Squizz gotta rabbit to shoot. Gun, Squizz!"

Squirrel grinned and darted off on his new errand. Brenna squatted on the woodland floor beside the hide. She was a year older than me, I decided, the same age as Ali and Blake, but in many ways she seemed ten years older at least.

"I hope you make it," she said. "Odds are against you but don't mean you won't win out. If you get away, proper away, lose yourself a long way from here, you can get away with it. You wouldn't be the first."

"Thanks," we said.

"Good luck to you," she said. "Get ya 'eads down. You look knackered. I'll knock you up later, we'll 'ave a drink."

She headed back through the brambles to join her younger brother. Ali and I crawled into the shelter; it was at once cool and cosy and beautifully silent. We stretched out under the blankets on the carpet of bark.

A blanket of black descended on us and we took maybe four hours of dreamless asleep. Night fell and Brenna was back, howling at our door, her breath fuggy and sweet with cider.

"All right lads, coming out to play?"

My eyes were glued together; I wanted to sleep for a thousand years, but she was not to be refused. She shook my shoulder roughly and when I groaned to let her know I didn't want to play. But she was having none of it.

"C'mon lads. Come see what's going on."

I groaned and turned over again. Ali was spark out beside me. Then I felt an acidic sweetness at my lips and realised Brenna was trying to pour cider into my mouth. I spluttered and gagged as it ran straight down my throat and choked me. I sat up.

"OK, OK... I'm awake. I'm awake."

"Good boy!" Brenna clapped me on the shoulder, produced another bottle of cider and efficiently cracked the cap off with her teeth. She handed it to me and clinked her own bottle enthusiastically against mine. Then she kicked Ali hard and, when Ali sat up confused and ready to fight, slapped an open bottle into his bemused hand too.

We followed Brenna's torch beam on to the thin path, through the clearing with the fire and finally to the top of the drop where we could see the site below us. In the night, it was transformed. The fire was enormous, the size of a small house, and glowed with shades of red, white, orange and purple. To one side of the fire, a mass of bodies, maybe 100 people, milled and wheeled to a raucous beat supplied by a group of ragged musicians armed with drums, violins and guitars. They were led by a skeletal violin player, grinning devilishly as he played faster and faster. We stopped to marvel at the crowd; it had all the activity of a market place with several stalls where travellers swapped bottles of cider and beer for cash. On its outskirts, men and women unbuttoned their clothes to piss into the night. I had never seen anything like it and I glanced at Ali, wondering if we should allow ourselves to be led into such a place.

Brenna had an impish grin, delighted to initiate us into the throng and we half walked, half slid down the bank towards the crowd. At its edge Brenna was stopped by a couple of lank-haired young men with broken teeth and large cider bottles.

"Little Brenna!" one exclaimed, attempting to drape a hand round her shoulder.

"Get your hands offa me Nadge ya git," she said, wriggling clear of the man's arm. Her tone was playful but steely. Nadge withdrew his arm. "Gis a smoke, Bim," she demanded of the other man and Bim instantly obeyed, reaching into his denim jacket pocket and producing a packet of Marlboros. He flicked the base and a couple of cigarettes popped out. Brenna took one with a flourish and lit it with the battered metal lighter she had used earlier.

"Who ya pals?" asked the first man, Nadge, with a trace of a sneer.

"This here's Rich and Al," said Brenna, "friends of mine."

Bim nodded and waved the packet under our noses and for the sake of appearances we took one each and let Brenna light us up. Immediately the acrid smoke got stuck in my throat and threatened to choke me and let loose a humiliating cough. Somehow I suppressed it, taking a swig of my cider bottle to counterbalance the dizziness. After that I got a method down for pretend smoking, just nipping at the fag and taking the smoke into my mouth rather than my lungs. Ali was doing the same but, luckily, the dark was masking our smoking incompetence.

"All right lads?" said Nadge evenly, "enjoying yourselves?"

We nodded and laughed, trying to fit in, and Brenna led us away, on through the dance floor where the crowd were thick, swaying and jostling to the beat of the fiddle player's demonic scratching. We ducked and weaved to prevent getting elbows in the face and, at the crowd's edge, took refuge in a cluster of hay bales to watch the dancers throw themselves around in the firelight. I took another large swig of the cider, getting a taste for it. The wave of nausea the cigarette had brought on had passed and, with the evil fag safely trodden into the mud of the dance floor, I was beginning to enjoy the sweet fizzy punch of the cider on the back of my throat. I turned to look at Ali and I could see he was alright too. We exchanged grins: we were having a good run.

"Here's to the road," I said, raising my bottle towards the sky.

"The road," agreed Brenna with enthusiasm.

"The road," said Ali and we clinked bottles. Then I saw a strangely familiar figure. He was standing at the edge of the dance floor, hat pulled over his eyes, swigging from a sherry bottle as he regarded the dancing with distaste. Belle stood attentively at his side. How could Wild Bill be here? I asked myself. And how could he be alive? My mind sped back to the copse and the hideous body cross with Bill at its head. Could he have survived? We hadn't looked at him in the copse as much as the others, as much as Shanklin, Physics and Mary that was true. Was he carrying the deaths of his friends around with him? Ruminating over death as he swigs from his bottle? I dug Ali hard in the ribs and pointed in Bill's direction but as I did a wave of leather jackets pushed towards the front and our view of Bill was cut off.

"What?" demanded Ali. I had probably given him a nasty jab.

I realised that letting on about our connection with Wild Bill in front of Brenna might raise complications and decided to keep stumm. "Nothing. Just those biker guys."

Actually, there was something to look at: a bit of a scuffle had broken out on the dance floor. One of the group of black leather-jacketed bikers had pushed one of the travellers, a lean drunkard with a hooknose and hair down to the small of his back, over onto the dirt floor. Too drunk to right himself immediately, he lay on the floor cursing and an outraged circle of his friends had moved to confront a severe looking man with a shaved head and a long beard. Two lines were forming: the bikers on one side and Arthur and his tribe of travellers on the other. Wild Bill faded into the shadows. I heard a soft click beside me; Brenna had her knife out. She cursed under her breath. Abruptly, the music lurched to a halt as the musicians looked to see what would happen. Only the desperate and incoherent shouts of drunks at the edge of the site far away from the fire could be heard.

Arthur stepped into the pool of quiet. His voice, clear and authoritative, but thick with menace. "This is a peaceful party. We're not wanting trouble here." There were a few sniggers from the line of bikers. An irreverent cough or two. "But if you want it, do not doubt that we will serve it to you. Who's your leader?"

A man in his early forties with distinguished grey hair and a strangely refined face stepped forward. He nodded ceremonially at Arthur. The issue was clear: neither party would back down and risk losing face. Were we about to witness more death?

"Newton?" exclaimed Arthur and the distinguished man nodded almost indiscernibly. "It's been a long time."

"Good evening, Arthur," said Newton. "It certainly has."

A little of the tension seemed to have gone. "You are welcome here, Newton," said Arthur, "but tell your boys to play nicely."

"No need to worry about that," said Newton with apparent sincerity, "my boys always play very nice."

The wave of bikers laughed nervously and a couple of the travellers grinned wryly. The crisis seemed to have been averted. Newton clapped hook nose on the back. "Our apologies," he said. "Shake his hand," he ordered the man with the pirate beard gruffly who immediately did as he was told. I heard another little click beside me: Brenna had folded her knife away.

The crowd began to talk again, trading comments in low voices. "Do you know him, that Newton?" I whispered to Brenna.

"Nah," she said. "But he won't mess with Arthur. No one does."

Then the sound of drunken singing broke through the crowd. It was a slurred but spirited rendition of 'Oh My Darling Clementine' and it was delivered by none other than Wild Bill. He meandered through the parting ranks, a showman to the last, singing softly and surprisingly tunefully into the faces of the travellers and the bikers.

Oh me darling, oh me darling
Oh me darling Clementine
Thou art lost and gone forever
Oh me darling Clementine

The band struck up, joining in with the refrain, and the party dissolved into laughter, the deadly tension of a few minutes earlier forgotten.

Ali gasped beside me. "We thought he was dead!"

"Who? Bill?" said Brenna with curiosity. "You know him?"

"A bit," said Ali. "We've met him before."

"We saw him and a bunch of drunks sprawled out in a field near Oxford," I explained. "Thought he was a dead man."

"Not Bill," said Brenna. "Constitution of an ox, Arthur says."

"Does he live here?" I asked.

"Nah. Bill don't live nowhere really. Although some say he's got a place Wallingford way. We see him sometimes. He comes and sleeps in Frankie's trailer, then he's gone again. No idea where to and no one can get any sense out of him neither, so no point asking him."

There was too much to think about, everything was uncertain. The euphoria of the cider hit had turned sour and made my head throb. As the party livened up again, I exchanged nods with Ali and we took our leave. Thanking Brenna and Squirrel for the bed and the cider, we picked our way back up the hill through the clearing and into the brambles where our nest waited for us. We lit a candle. In the distance we could hear the droning wild music churning out into the night and the whoops and catcalls of drunken revellers. It had been quite a night.

"Bill's alive," I said.

"I know," said Ali. We were both strangely thankful for this, a slight lessening of our burden, our terrible shared secrets.

"What about the others?" I asked.

"I don't know. Physics had his eyes open. You can't sleep with your eyes open. I don't know..." I saw Ali shake his head in the candlelight.

Minutes passed. We watched a moth dance around the flame in front of us. Finally I said it.

"Blake?"

"No, he's definitely gone," said Ali and I noticed a tear running down the side of his face from the corner of his eye.

"What?" I asked gently.

"Nothing." He shook his emotions away. "I'm glad I did what I did. I'd do it again too." I nodded gently, encouraging him to open up. He shook his head again, as if trying to allow the mess in his head to settle. "Why aren't the police after us, Rich?"

"I don't know but I think we can disappear, Ali. Look at Bill. No one knows who he is or where he comes from. We can be like that."

We brooded on it in silence: the terrible life of the free and the nameless. Eventually the flame died and we fell gratefully back into the arms of deep and dreamless sleep.

Nine

THE ISLAND AND THE MEAT

Dogs. Relentless barking. Intruding on my sleep, nudging me awake. I gathered my blanket around my ears to block out the noise. Too loud; too intense. Suddenly awake with fear in my belly and my throat, eyes wide open. Ali staring at me across the hide, teeth bared, bracing himself. It was dawn. Grey, hazy light leaked into our shelter like smoke. Now we could hear shouts, the clang and clatter of metal on metal. We understood together what was happening: the site was under attack.

And we knew what we had to do. We had to get out. It was time to go, time to go again. Alarm bells rang in our heads. I peered out of the shelter. No one there; no one coming. All the noise was coming from the site. Ali appeared beside me, blinking in the half-light.

"What's happening?"

"It's the site, the police, maybe. We need to go."

But we couldn't go, couldn't run without taking a look first. We retraced the previous day's steps, passing the clearing and breaking through the trees to where the ground fell away and we could see the site again. An untidy row of police vanshad lined up. Uniforms herded their occupants out of their tatty vans and converted buses. Mindless barking filled the air; the seething police dogs and the panicked travellers' hounds yelped and snarled at one another. As we watched, a baton swung, a wing mirror smashed and two men moved forward, fists raised. And a group of uniforms waded in, swinging their weapons, driving the men back, forcing them to the ground. We saw it.

Then we picked out Brenna. She was waving her blade menacingly at a clutch of uniforms moving purposefully towards her, heads bent, crouching, eyes locked on their quarry. Squirrel emerged from a van behind the policemen and leapt onto the back of their leader like a crazed wild cat, tearing at his hair and biting his throat. We could hear the copper holler and scream as his friends tore Squirrel away, taking clumps of hair with him. Meanwhile, Brenna seized her moment and lunged forward with her blade. But she didn't look behind her and see another officer advancing with a raised baton. She took a blow across the shoulders and fell; the blade was prised from her grip and she and Squirrel are folded and pressed onto the floor. I feel Ali shift beside me. "They need our help," he mumbled.

"We can't. We'll be caught too."

I saw Ali nod. He knew I was right. We watched in desperation as the incident with Brenna and Squirrel was repeated all over the site; there were dozens of arrests and soon the prisoners, hands cuffed behind them, were being led away. Then I spotted another uniform, talking into a walkie-talkie and looking our way long and hard. He barked into his radio urgently.

We ran fast and hard through the woods, back towards Radley. At the path where we had met Brenna and Squirrel we saw blue lights ahead, white steel panels. They had blocked our escape route, closing off the rat runs in case any travellers were to try and run out that way. The dawning of an idea emerged. Were they looking for us? Without exchanging a word, our telepathy sharp, we turned together away from the vans and ran hard away on an animal path leading away from the site and the road. Eventually we reached a wooden fence at the forest's edge with a long grass meadow stretching out beyond it.

We stood panting with our hands holding our knees as we surveyed the meadow in front of us. It was overgrown with waist-high green grass, running for a hundred yards or so before abruptly ending in a stone wall about 12 feet high. There was no sign of the police but we knew if we broke out across the field we would be exposed, caught with nowhere to run.

"What do we do?" Ali shook his head and we surveyed the scene again. I made out an imposing oak next to the wall. From where we stood it looked like its branches might stretch promisingly close to the wall. "We could get over that wall, I think." Ali nodded. In the distance we heard the distant yelp of dogs and remembered the carnage we were running from. It was time to take a chance.

We sprinted across the field full pelt, the wet, long grass lashing at our ankles. If the police saw us, we would be finished. But we reached the wall undetected. Our palms slammed against its rough, cold surface and we got to work on the tree. Ali hitched me up so I could grasp one of the lower limbs, hoist myself up and lie across one of the great branches. It was as broad as a barrel, strong and reassuring. I reached down with both arms and pulled up the rucksacks; my hands could just get hold of Ali's who was standing on tiptoe against the trunk. I pulled him up and we were safe amongst the leaves.

From the safety of the branch we could see the reason for the wall. We were overlooking a large house surrounded by tidy gardens and a vegetable patch. It was an English country mansion, a setting for a murder mystery or a Victorian romance. The house itself was a chocolate box cube, French windows and patio doors set in smart limestone, decked in vines and creepers. Tennis courts and a swimming pool completed the picture. We squinted at it longingly. It was too perfect to be simply someone's house. Maybe, I thought, it was an upmarket hotel, some sort of celebrity retreat or stately home. We marvelled at the perfection of it, its arrogance.

"Do you think we should get down?" Ali asked.

I didn't see we had much choice. True, we might trap ourselves if we did. But we couldn't go back to the field, couldn't stay in the tree and it seemed unlikely the police would come looking for us or anyone here. If we could get out of sight. I didn't answer but instead crawled towards where the branch touched the top of the wall and swung my feet onto the wall. I felt the heavy branch bend back upwards towards Ali as I shifted my weight off it. Then, keeping an eye on the silent house, and holding onto smaller branches to steady myself, I transferred myself entirely to the wall. My eyes stayed trained on the house, searching for any sign, any movement that signalled that our presence had been detected. Nothing. All remained still within. The walls had been buttressed with sloping brick supports, an easy way down, and also a quick way out. I clambered gently to the ground. Ali followed and we were soon standing at the edge of a vegetable patch, blinking in the brilliant morning sunshine. Still. All was quiet.

We crept alongside some beanpoles framing leafy sprouts towards the house. We were famished: nothing to eat since Brenna's stew yesterday lunch and on the run and living off our wits for three days and nights, we had morphed into sleek predators. I flushed with pride as I stole a look at Ali who was moving behind a long potting shed. He looked lean, feral, sharpened by hunger and adrenalin. The world was opening up before us, a picture book of possibilities and adventures. Our lives in Oxford, school, home, the gang, shrunk before the animal thrill of life on the run.

We approached the house through a vegetable garden, hoping to find an unattended kitchen. There were herbs in large clay pots surrounding the door and we each grabbed handfuls of parsley and munched. Then, tentatively, we tested the brass knob of the door. Locked but still no sound. Braver now, like emboldened jackals, we circled the house. At head height, a window was ajar, small but possible for our bony frames. Ali lifted me up and I climbed through. A cistern in front of me and I realised I was entering a toilet. Good news. I dropped soundlessly to the floor, bolted the door and pulled Ali inside, standing on the toilet seat. It was an old fashioned room, clean but worn with heavy porcelain and faded chequered linoleum. I eased back the bolt, opened the door and peered out at a corridor decorated with staid, stuffy grandeur: a grey carpet ran like a canal over bitumen stained floorboards; there were faded fleur de leys on the wallpaper and archaic light switches. A vague smell of disinfectant hung in the air and in the distance we could just make out what sounded like the drone of a distorted television set. We looked at one another and, with our packs still on our backs, crept down the corridor away from the television noise towards a glimmer of natural light spilling onto a hallway floor.

We arrived at what seemed to be the prep room of a hotel kitchen. Clear scrubbed aluminium worktops surrounded us, beneath our feet was a grey vinyl floor and to our right a bank of fridges. As we took it in, a sudden movement to our left startled us and we froze, peering towards another section of the kitchen as a burly figure in chef's whites appeared carrying an enormous stock pot. Stunned, we watched as, with his back to us, he hauled the pot onto a range, turned and went out of sight again without taking us in. He broke into a whistle, an absent half-tune, as he moved towards what must have been a door to the outside. We drew backwards in the direction we had arrived from, but, as we did, Ali stopped and eased open one of the fridges. Inside there were metal trays of some indiscernible food, probably meat, wrapped in white plastic. Ali took a bag, a great bulky thing the size of a sack of potatoes. Its contents settled inside the bag as he hugged it to his chest and a few drops of blood dropped onto the vinyl floor. Meat. Now we had hunted we withdrew.

I gently tried the handle of the toilet door. Nothing gave. I had another go. The door was locked from the inside. In the time it had taken us to make a brief visit to the kitchen and return to the toilet, someone had got in and locked the door behind them. The house was creeping and contracting with unexpected life.

"Hang on." We stepped away from the door in horror. The voice from inside was male, gruff, Scottish, not old, not young. Then there was clatter and the sound of pouring water from the kitchen. We didn't have much choice but to steal away into the guts of the house.

We reached a square, open hallway, both grand and squalid with a dark low ceiling and the stainless steel doors of a lift ahead of us. There were options here: a wider corridor led off to the right and steps descended to what looked like a doorway to our left. A shout rang out from the kitchen, maybe from the chef we'd seen. "Tony, that you? Give us a hand with these spuds will you?"

Instinctively we moved towards the doorway, the only direction from which no life was closing in on us. But as we made our way towards the door a crack appeared and a female hand struggled to take her key out of the latch and keep hold of her handbag. We had to pace away sharpish down the second corridor, towards the TV drone. There was a recess immediately on our right with a large plant in front of it and we squeezed in there with our packs on our backs pressed to the wall. We knew we were going to get cornered at any moment.

"Tony?" The chef again. He had found the woman. "Oh, Marg, seen Tony?"

"No, I haven't. And a very good morning to you too." The playfully severe voice of some kind of boss housemaid.

"Sorry. Morning. Just thought I heard..."

"Where's Jimmy? Ah..."

"Morning all." And here was the Scotsman, emerging from our toilet. "Don't be going in there for some time now."

We moved on under cover of their laughter. Up ahead a burst of canned laughter sounded out again. The television we heard earlier was up ahead and someone was watching a comedy show. Behind us, doors were slamming, several young women could be heard chattering. Workers were arriving to begin their shift. We were sure to be discovered soon. We reached the door to the room with the loud TV. Just as we got there, heard male voices and footsteps on the polished wooden floor coming towards the hallway. We were pincered and had to duck into the TV room.

It was a large room with a dark pink carpet and several armchairs pointing towards the TV. A large bay window looked out across the driveway towards a gate. Two cars were driving in: now we knew we were trapped and I started to think about the police again, their enquiries, the body, Blake's body. This might be our last stand. With nowhere left to hide and nothing to lose, we sat down in a couple of the armchairs in front of the TV, Ali still holding the dripping bag of meat. I calculated the odds of us making it if we hurled ourselves through the glass in the bay window or if we rushed the workers in the corridor. Not good. The closing credits of an American sitcom were playing and, stupidly, the armchair I had dodged into felt lovely comfortable. Despite the summer heat, this place had the central heating on and the dry heat was driving my eyelids closed. Then Ali tapped my arm and pointed towards a chair two down from where we were sitting. Folded up inside it was an impossibly, small, frail old man in a purple dressing gown. He was looking at us `with an encouraging, gummy grin. Not knowing what else to do, we grinned back.

Then a burst of brass: a news bulletin began. Angela Rippon, Elvis Presley rolling fat hips in sparkly white suit. Flowers. Elvis dead. Memphis. More flowers. Tearful fans. More footage of the man on stage. I didn't really care. Ali and I were outside the world then, locked out, bigger fish to fry. The gummy man beside us stared at the TV, a shrunken child. He didn't seem to care much either.

"Mr. French?" Marg, the housemaid, was in the room! We were ready for it now, the struggle, the arrest. We just waited like condemned men. We could have bolted past Marg back into the corridor, I suppose, or maybe even leapt through the window onto the drive. But neither felt remotely possible. We just waited for them to come and take us away.

"Yes, dear?" Mr French's voice had surprising resonance and authority.

"Elvis' funeral." said Marg fondly, "Don't show Jimmy. He'll get upset."

"I wouldn't dream of it." We turned our heads towards Mr French. His tiny, bony body, folded in purple towelling, was like a bird's skeleton encased in cotton wool. Then we grinned with delight. He had given us a heavy conspiratorial wink!

"He can't hear anyway." Marg was off, her voice fading as she moved towards the door. "He's got the radio on. When do you want your breakfast, Mr French?"

"Not straight away, dear, get yourself settled first."

"Thank you, Mr French. Will you manage a poached egg this morning?"

"Yes, dear, I believe I will. But no hurry now." This little man was protecting us. I glanced at Ali, and flashed him a quick grin. We might make it after all.

With Marg out of it, we turned back to the news: the Queen was out and about meeting troops, men in suits, children; a man in an Arab headdress sitting in front of about a thousand microphones; and the earth was parched, cracked dry, dry river beds, sacks of potatoes loaded onto flatbed trucks and then suddenly there we were. Ali and me, side by side on the screen. We gasped in horror and astonishment and looked startled at one another and then at Mr French; but he just grinned at us again.

"The hunt for the missing Oxford boys, Richard Turner

and Alistair Johnston, has widened. Police forces across the country are looking for the boys who disappeared from their homes during Thursday evening and have not been seen since. Police are anxious to get in touch with anyone who has seen them or may be able to help find them."

Our faces were still frozen on the screen, painfully exposed. Ali's picture was his annual school shot from last September but my shot was more recent; it was from a photograph mum had taken the month before. It was a portrait: Beth, Rachel and me in the garden staring moodily at the lens. Snapped under duress. The coppers had got hold of it though, cut me out and blown my stupid noggin up so much I looked like a bursting orange. But it was still definitely me.

Mr. French was still staring at the screen. The news ended and, hearing nothing from the corridor, we got up and waved an apologetic goodbye to our host. He just gummy grinned back: a proper gent. We heard voices coming from the kitchen as we crept back along the corridor but we were quick and silent as we tiptoed out into the morning, emerging at a corner of the house where the driveway gave way to a lawn bordered by rhododendrons, Ali still holding his sagging parcel of meat.

We took cover in the flowers, squeezed the meat into Ali's pack and scrambled up the buttresses and away over the wall. Then we were back into the long grass and we followed the wall south until it ended, then moved through fields and hedges, oblivious to obstacles, until the river opened up before us again. We had outlived the king of rock and roll. We would survive.

We tramped the path skirting the Thames for a mile or two, our hunger fading as the heat of the day ramped up again. We loosened our jackets and rolled up our jeans and headed south. We were searching for real sanctuary, a bolthole of the quality of the nook, somewhere to hide out for the day away from curious eyes. Then we would walk again when night fell.

The island was a clump of trees and bushes that looked

like it had fallen out of the sky and landed in the middle of the river. From the bank where we stood looking longingly at it, it wasn't clear whether there was any actual land there at all. The Thames was wide there, maybe 50 feet across, and the island was sitting where the river opened out even wider as it turned a corner on its slow amble to London.

"Can we swim there?" asked Ali.

"I think so," I said and began to get undressed. The banks were clear but it wouldn't be long before someone came along: we needed shelter. We stripped to our pants and stuffed our clothes into our packs. Then we waded into the river holding the bags above our heads to keep our things dry. Three metres in the oozing mud beneath our feet gave way and we struggled to keep the bags clear of our heads as the tide tightened its grip around us. We failed: everything got soaked by the time we reached the island's shore. There was more mud there but beyond that firm ground, a natural clearing, secluded and shady. Perfect. We startled a flock of ducks and they fussed off as we took hold of their hideaway.

In the island's centre, raw sunshine broke through the trees and here we spread our sopping things out to dry. I looked at my stopped watch again. I considered throwing it away but instead spread it out to dry, a futile gesture since I knew it was broken for good. And time had stopped anyway, or felt like it had. We opened up the pack of meat. Diced steak, looking fresh, bright and moist. Ravenous, we examined the flesh.

"You can eat meat raw, can't you?" said Ali.

"Beef yes." I remembered the shock of burgers raw and spongy in France. They had tasted good and juicy.

So we set about the meat. The little cubes were chewy but they tasted good. I wrapped mine in dock leaves, making little parcels like spring rolls. I told Ali he should try his red with a bit of green but he just chewed carefully on the flesh, wringing out every bit of goodness and the flavour. We finished half the bag quickly and, feeling full, rewrapped the rest of the beef in the bag and tucked it away in the shade. Then we stretched out alongside our clothes in the sun. We were perfectly hidden. The grind of an outboard motor passed on the river but we were stashed safe, out of sight.

"Nice here," I said.

"We could just live here."

Maybe we could, I thought, for a while. But how would we eat? We couldn't carry out raids on the big house regularly; it was only by luck that we had managed to escape with the meat. And I remembered the news bulletin. We were famous. What would our friends be thinking? Our parents? A shard of regret shot through me: my mother had lost a child, she would be wringing with worry and suffering. But I was here, I thought, I was safe, I was strong.

"One day it will rain," I said. "We need to be somewhere proper by then."

Ali looked around the island and we both saw then that it wasn't anywhere proper. It was a dream and as temporary as one too.

"My dad will know what to do," said Ali, "We'll decide when we get there."

"Will he?" There was a hint of dissent in my voice and I didn't know where it had come from. It startled us both. Ali propped himself up on one elbow and looked at me levelly.

"Yes, he will."

"Won't he just turn us in?"

Ali considered this carefully. "I don't know. If he does, then that's the right thing."

I could feel frustration building. "But it's not necessarily the right thing though. Blake died because..." Words failed me.

"Because he was a ... bastard?"

"Yes!"

"So?"

"So we shouldn't have to suffer for it then. We need to

take control. Make our own life."

"If that's right, then Dad'll know it."

My irritation burst. "But why will he know? Dads don't know everything. They don't. My dad was OK but he wouldn't know what to do about this. And now he's gone and we survived without him. I survive. And I'm OK."

Ali sounded like he was going to considerable effort to control his temper. His voice was flat and even, but hard. "Richard, you don't know..."

"What do you mean? I..."

Ali cut me dead. "You didn't kill him, did you?"

And he was right; I hadn't. If we were caught, Ali was going to be charged with something, murder, manslaughter, I didn't know what. But I was innocent. I did not push Blake into the lock and what's more I tried to save him as well. There was the difference between us. I was on the run and enjoying the thrill of the adventure but ultimately I had nothing to lose: if we were caught the worst I could expect was some sort of telling off by the law and the gaining of a reputation as a heroic adventurer. I would be free to bask in that as the memory faded and I went back to a normal life. It would not be the same for Ali. He would have to live with what he had done forever.

But maybe we had killed him together, I thought, the two of us. Just two nights had passed since that fatal moment on the canal bank but already it seemed an age away. First of all, so much had happened, meeting Brenna and Squirrel, the traveller site and the ghost of Wild Bill turning up, the police raid and the meat thieving at the mansion. But there was more than that: the moment at the lock seemed to be distorting, flexing, opening up for interpretation.

"I told you to do it," I said. "I said go on Ali and you punched him and he fell in. You didn't know, we didn't know, he couldn't swim."

Ali looked at me. I could see he was replaying the horror

of the moment in his mind too.

"How come he just sank? People don't drown like that, do they? They struggle, don't they?"

"Unless you knocked him cold..." I said, realising too late I had just made it worse.

Ali shuddered and then nodded slowly. "I need to ask my dad," he said again and this time I didn't argue.

Laughing and chattering floated over from the bank then: a party of passing walkers, not 40 feet from where we were. We listened carefully, tuning into the conversation like spies scanning a radio dial. Fragments of normal life: a pub at Dorchester, a daughter's progress at University, wild flowers in the hedgerow.

"It's an island," said a fruity disembodied voice, a middle-aged male, not a professional tour guide but one of those annoying blokes who thinks he knows everything. "Now. They say that King John..."

"Ah, the bad guy in Robin Hood?" chucked in a sprightly female voice to knowing laughter.

"The same. Well, after a bit of struggle he was basically forced to stop being such a bugger." More laughter. "...And sign the Magna Carta. In ...1215 this was, and some people... well it's clearly not right but anyway...some people think he signed it right there on that island."

We imagined them all gathered on the bank, looking appreciatively at our hiding place.

"Well, if you hear that, don't believe it. The truth is he absolutely could not have because actually the island was created in 1835!" More appreciative laughter.

"Come on then," said a third voice, another man's. "If we listen to any more of Michael's interesting facts, we shall miss lunch."

And then they were gone and, reassured by the sounds of normality, we rolled back into the shade and drifted off into daydreams.

"We leave tonight," said Ali sleepily, "Rest today and walk in the dark. Safer that way."

We set off after night fell. We woke at dusk and shared another meal of raw beef and dock leaf, then waited until a sliver of moon rose and there was enough light to see by. Then we gathered our things into our packs. I considered throwing away the watch, the grisly reminder of our crime, but in the end I stashed it at the bottom of my pack. We couldn't afford to leave any traces. This time we didn't risk trying to carry our bags through the water and instead waded out into the river in our underpants and hurled the bags onto the river path. We felt pleased with ourselves: military tight, alert and ready for the next stage of our journey. We dressed quietly as the water ghosted by our feet, and then set off along its path.

We hiked a few miles, passing the lights of villages and creeping past the occasional riverside cottage. Abingdon approached, lightening streaked the sky, the orange haze of streetlight ahead. We crossed the crowded apron of a busy pub, its terrace chock full of gabbling drinkers clutching glasses of beer and wine. But we were invisible now, and inscrutable too, foxes with well honed skills, tuned to evade our hunters. We simply walked casually through the good-humoured crowd, heads down, purposeful. No one said a thing. The pub garden ended in some steps that rose to the edge of a busy road that crossed the river at the town's borders. We crossed the bridge and dropped onto the quiet dark side of the river to continue our journey and eavesdrop on the life on the other bank.

More miles, silently marched in the dark and then we rounded a bend to see the lights of another riverside pub ahead. This one was different from the last: a few quiet drinkers collected around wooden tables on the banks of the river, nursing meditative pints and cigarettes. They were older than the last pub crowd, less self-absorbed: we knew we would not pass unnoticed this time. I realised suddenly that apart from a few people in Radley, the travellers and the old man, we had successfully avoided all face-to-face contact. That's why we were still at large; after all we were national news and people must have been on the lookout for us. The path ahead of us threaded between the river and the idle gaze of a garden full of summer drinkers. It was too risky, too quiet; we would have to skirt around the front of the pub and rejoin the path beyond it.

It was reasonably easy to execute this plan and we emerged back in the dark with the distant hubbub of drinking chatter receding as we crept off back, quietly pleased with another successful manoeuvre.

"Richard." My name ringing out in the dark, in a kind of strangled stage whisper. We turned back towards the pub. No one was there. But the whisper came again and we realised then where it was coming from: from over the black sheen of the water. The Thames was wide there, spanning 40 feet bank to bank, but just where we were then it rounded a tight couple of turns to form a horseshoe and, at this spot, as it cornered, the far bank was less than half its usual width. We stared across the river's murky surface. On the far bank, a man was standing, silhouetted in the moonlight. He shone a strong flashlight on the ground by his trainers to mark his position and to let us know he had it. A knot bunched up in my guts. "Don't be afraid, Richard," said Macaulay, clearer, more confident now he had our attention, "I'm not going to hurt you. I can't reach you after all. I only want to speak with you."

"It's him," I hissed at Ali, "Macaulay, the bent policeman." We stared out across the black water.

"It's very important that I speak to you," Macaulay urged. "Is that Ali with you there? You boys must be very scared."

Ali and I looked at one another. "We're not scared," called out Ali.

"I know, I know," purred Macaulay. "But still, I can help

you, if you let me."

Ali squinted across the water, no doubt he was making the same calculations I had. Was this a trap? I didn't see how it could be. We had not passed a bridge over the river for a few miles back, nothing since before Abingdon. Ahead, we didn't know but there was nothing in sight. He could have launched himself into the river it was true but we would have been long gone by the time he reached us. We were safe: he could talk to us but he couldn't touch us. Still, we both glanced into the copse to our left, calculating how quickly we could escape into the darkness if we needed to. Pretty quickly. In any case, we felt safe, relaxed enough to be curious.

"What do you want?" called Ali. He sounded confident, in control.

"You must need help." Macaulay's voice was soft in the night; this was a different side to the drill sergeant that had plucked me from the rec three nights ago. It was still him though. And he was still dangerous.

"How did you find us?" Ali was managing the conversation and I was glad. My emotions were tangled: fear, hatred, contempt, and somewhere deep in the mix, I didn't know why this was, and it was somehow more disturbing than the other feelings, there was comfort too.

"Luck," he said, "I guessed you might head south but... I've been looking for you, driving around, keeping my eyes open. And I've something the police don't, I trust my instincts. Their search is all..." He paused to search for a missing word then spat it out with contempt: "Procedure! They have to have a method. A couple of intelligent boys like yourselves can easily outwit them and their clumsy systems, but I don't have to justify myself to anyone. I just listen to my instincts and they usually turn out be correct."

"You are the police," said Ali.

"I'm not an ordinary policeman. I..." Macaulay paused, searching for the right words. He moved right to the lip of the bank. "I am special agent you might say. Anyway I'm not here to turn you into the authorities. Trust me on that at least."

This was confusing. I half wished we had turned and ran when we first clocked him.

"Richard, look," he muttered, barely audible over the river. He seemed to be frustrated and balled a fist. Then he raised his voice a notch. "I made a mistake," he called out clearly, "I let you get the idea that something..." He struggled for words. "...Something improper might have been happening. I think we both know it didn't. I..."

"What do you want?" cut in Ali.

"Where are you heading boys? You cannot run for ever. You have to stop eventually."

"None of your business."

"You don't need to worry. I told you, I've no interest in turning you in. But I could help you, if you'll let me."

"No chance," said Ali.

"Very well then. Can you remember numbers? Remember these: Five one zero four two. Zero in the middle and both sides add up to six. Your house numbers, 15 and 24. Turn them backwards put a zero in the middle. That's my number, Oxford 51042, call me when you need me."

With that he turned and set off away from the river. We stared at one another in bemusement.

"Think it's a trap?" said Ali.

"Not sure."

"We need to get away from the river. They'll be looking for us here now. Unless..."

"He doesn't tell them."

"He'll be back to look for us anyway."

I nodded. It was true. And there was one more thing.

"He didn't mention Blake," I said.

"I know," said Ali. A glimmer of hope. Maybe George didn't squeal, maybe Blake had survived. But how? How?

We ran again, with survival in our legs and our lungs. We

crossed the river north of Appleford and clambered onto the silent iron sides of a rail bridge. The rail track felt like an old friend and we followed it towards the village until another friend, a dirty clump of buddleia, welcomed us. We picked our way to its centre and protected ourselves within its leaves for another night. Ali seemed to go straight to sleep but, lying next to him listening to his breath getting even and regular, I couldn't quite drop off. I wasn't cold and the earth bed underneath me felt surprisingly soft but my hand quivered a little and my teeth clenched. I realised it was anger that was keeping me awake. Anger at Macaulay, with his policeman act and his confusing offers of help. It was his fault, this mess that had cast me into a hedge miles from home. A chain of events started by him at the rec. His interference: our flight and our slaughter of Blake. His fault. But I had his number now. Five one zero four two. Zero in the middle and both sides add up to six. Our house numbers, 15 and 24. Turn them backwards put a zero in the middle. Somehow I knew it would be the key to finding our way back home, I just didn't know how yet.

Safe in that realisation, I finally drifted off to sleep.

Ten

MURDER BOY

In the morning we made tracks fast and hard south. Efficient now; method down. Fast by the rails, and when we heard the train, we ducked out of sight, then jumped out again, legs propelling us ever forward. We were above throwing stuff at the trains now; that had been games for children and we were grown up now. Crouched in hedges, we watched them pass. Once or twice, we traded a smile back and forth. Maybe, I thought, Ali was remembering the nook, the clay bombs, but we didn't need to talk about it anymore. Those boys were gone: one dead and two left running. But we followed the path of the trains, grateful for their route south, and for their shelter.

We reached the town of Didcot, its giant cooling towers keeping watch over clusters of modern houses, and stayed close to the tracks. We were not taking any care about being recognised at this point; we were walking angry, angry with the hand of fate. I guess we looked like two ordinary kids, two scruffy urchins lolling along by the tracks on another sunny morning, another day in another hot summer in crumbling old England. Two lads, unlikely to attract attention and the story of the missing boys getting old as well, disappearing off the news agenda. Gone four nights: one in the nook, one by the river, one with the travellers and one in a bush by the tracks. We were half asleep but despite our fatigue we were warriors, kings of the road, bloodied with death and hardening into survivors, tough nuts, far from the boys that ran horrified from the scene of the death. Now we knew we would survive.

We left Didcot with the tracks on our right. To our left a play park emerged spotted with infants and bored mothers. That gave way to a sprawling network of dusty football pitches, neglected in the tired heat. Following the line of the tracks, we saw the pitches end ahead and, beyond a fence with a gate, a wood beginning. Then we noticed a group of kids, our age, maybe older, Chelsea and Liverpool football tops, fags on the go, drifting off the fields towards the path ahead of us. They had noticed us too. Ali and I stayed quiet but our strides stiffened slightly and adrenaline fizzed in our stomachs. Striding casually up onto the path, the boys moved to position themselves in front of us at the gate, between the brambles at the edge of the embankment and a drop onto the expanse of pitches spreading out to our right. They took up position around the gate, exaggeratedly relaxed, casually spitting and smoking. I glanced at Ali but his eyes were fixed ahead. He must have known what was coming, I thought, but he didn't check his pace, kept moving hard ahead. There were four of them so we were outnumbered and, as we drew closer, I could gauge the characters and the dynamics. The leader, in Liverpool red, stood a little off the others, smoking as if taking sips of cool lemonade. He was their Blake, I realised, but older, darker. His underlings blocked our way more obviously. One was taller than all of us, us and his friends, but his loose jaw and soft skin marked him out as a raw youngster, a stooge. We slowed to a halt and the three kids in our way sneered.

"You letting us through then?" said Ali, a smile ghosting on his lips.

"Where you going?" said a lad with a face full of freckles, standing side on right in the gate. He glanced over his right shoulder towards the woods. "Nothing that way for you."

"Reading," said Ali. "We're heading for Reading."

The group leered at one another, all except their leader who stared mournfully at us still sip smoking. Heading for Reading, they sing-songed, mocking, glancing at one another and us, weighing up any threat we might offer. Only Sip Smoker stayed quiet. Then. "Badge," he said softly.

Ali had a small Leeds badge discreetly positioned on the breast of his jacket. I had not even noticed it before.

"That's a shit badge," said the tall boy. "Shit badge, shit team."

The third boy, crew cut and Chelsea shirt, caught my eye. He was the weak one, the George. I stared back, giving him nothing to work with.

Sip Smoker ground his fag out. "Take that badge," he instructed the tall lad.

Ali talked direct to Sip Smoker, bypassing his minions. "I'll fight you for it," he said. "You win, you take the badge; I win, I take your shirt." There was a moment of incredulous silence. My heart sank. This was a deadly, high stake gamble on Ali's part and I couldn't see how it would pay off. "And when I beat you," he said slowly, throwing in everything, "I'll take your shitty shirt and wipe my arse on it."

Sip Smoker's gang were waiting to see what their leader would do next. His impervious front was breached, he hesitated, calculating the odds. Ali stared him down.

Sip Smoker crouched slightly like a bull in the ring, gathering his strength. "Who are you?" he growled.

"I'm your murderer, son," said Ali quietly. I stole a glance at my friend. I hardly recognised my amiable, easy-going friend from Oxford. He stood taut, ready but relaxed, adopting a boxer's crouch, ready for, anticipating Sip Smoker's fists. His gaze bored into his opponent. Now the boy in the Liverpool shirt was recalculating, perhaps, he thought, he had met a proper tough, a boy to give him the hiding he had coming for a while. He glanced at the gaggle of kids he had in tow. Nothing there. I had stared down Chelsea shirt and moved onto freckle face. Almost imperceptibly, the boy edged aside from the gate opening, leaving our way clear. The tall boy's head dropped. All Sip Smoker needed was an honourable way out.

"What's ahead mate?" Ali gestured to the woods, as if the issue was now settled, over. He even offered Sip Smoker a conciliatory smile. It was a simple question but it carried meaning. What do you want to do? It asked. Make the right decision, it urged.

Disarmed, Sip hesitated. He cleared his throat. "Not much. There's a gypsy camp," he mumbled.

"Thanks mate," said Ali. He looked hard at the boy, a confident grin on his chops. "Could be just what we're looking for."

Sip Smoker smiled weakly. He would tell anyone later he tangled with a couple of gypsy boys, psychos, carrying a knife. The others wouldn't spoil his story, not for many years, not until it didn't matter anymore. They had reputations to protect too.

We walked past the boys coolly. But when we were deep in the folds of the wood we burst out into laughter. But I was looking at my friend in a new light. He was changing, growing into a role. And I wasn't sure I liked it.

A few miles on we found a camp. It was nothing like the site at Radley, a sad little cluster of vans around a small smouldering fire. We looked at one another, thinking the same thing.

"Think we'll find Brenna?" I said.

"Maybe."

"She helped us once."

"Yes but..."

"The police," I finished his sentence for him again. We were thinking as one. Had they been looking for us when they raided the site?

"Come on," I said and headed off in the direction of the trucks. We needed to reach out to the world, we were its problem and we would not go away. 100 yards off the vans barking started up; a couple of Alsatians broke out from the shade and bound towards us, yapping and snarling. We held our hands up, cooing and calling softly to the beasts. They stopped a few yards from us and bared their teeth, growling menacingly.

"What'd ya want?" A woman in her late twenties, an older Brenna, hard stare, head scarf, filthy combats.

"Do you know Brenna?" I said and she looked at us quizzically. "Brenna," I repeated, "She's got a brother called Squirrel. They're friends of ours."

A man joined the woman. He was young, lean, with long hair, a wispy beard and a black eye. A veteran of the attack, maybe? He called off the dogs impatiently and they sulked away in disgrace. He looked at us suspiciously. "Brenna and Squirrel McGuire you say you're looking for?" he asked.

It had to be them. How many people are called Brenna? Or Squirrel? "Yes. Them."

"They're not here."

"Do you know where they are?"

He looked at us hard, scrutinising, sizing us up. "You're the kids the filth are looking for, aren't you?"

"No..."

"There's a lot of us reckon Radley got turned over 'cos of you. Plenty would skin you alive for bringing the filth on us."

We stood speechless, waiting for something to give. We were at their mercy. Eventually the woman's gaze softened. "It's not their fault, Jed," she said.

He shrugged. "Didn't say it was. Anyway Arthur's kids aren't here so..."

"Take them over to Arthur."

He let loose a low whistle. "Arthur'll kill 'em."

"He won't." But she looked doubtful.

Jed looked at us with mild exasperation, unsure of what to do. "I'll take 'em," he said finally. "Drop 'em at the site and they can do what they like. Don't want them here, that's for sure."

The woman nodded and Jed turned and disappeared. Once he went she gave us a proper smile. "Don't know what you've done and I don't care. You look all right to me."

We grinned inanely back and a car started up. Jed appeared beside us at the wheel of a wrecked chocolate brown Cavalier. We jumped in the back, Jed growled at us to get down out of sight and we crouched low in the filthy vinyl seats. The dogs clambered in through the front passenger window and one, hot and heavy with pants and slobber, settled between us. Finally, the woman leant in through an open passenger window and solemnly pressed bread rolls with onion, salad and a strange soft cheese into our hands. We thanked her and we were off, roaring through country lanes with throbbing hypnotic rock music screaming from his car stereo. Before we knew it, he had pulled up on the verge of a lane and was pointing back towards the way we came.

"Back there is a gate. Cross the field and you'll reach Arthur's site. Don't blame me if he rips yer little heads off and don't, whatever you do, mention that I brought you here."

We staggered out of the car and Jed was gone, leaving us blinking on the verge.

We did as he said, but first we ate the rolls. Delicious; more sustenance from the people who live on the road. We knew we owed them and, silently, I vowed that someday I would repay their kindness. We passed through the gate and saw another dull parched field ahead of us. Smoke rose in one corner above a clump of oaks and we saw the tell-tale battered plate metal sides of the trucks. Another site, Arthur's and therefore Brenna and Squirrel's. We needed to be careful, Arthur would kill us, Jed wasn't joking, and we remembered the hulking figure with the tattoos and the pony tail, the man who tamed Newton and his thuggish bikers. We needed to be careful all right. We edged round the field towards the plume of smoke, hoping to find Brenna without attracting the attention of the adults. There was no need to worry; she found us first.

A twig cracking underfoot and a stone hit me on the shoulder. This time the sharp pain was a relief. No ceremony this time: Brenna and Squirrel standing grimly before us, materialising out of a hedgerow, stern faced, no smiles.

"You can't come here," said Brenna, "I told you that before."

We nodded. We understood. We were trouble; we brought trouble to these people.

"Nothing personal," continued Brenna as Squirrel stood gravely in attendance, "but Arthur won't have it. We took a big hit yesterday. Family's split up, weakened. Word is the filth were looking for you. You'll have to go."

"Can't you help us at all?" chipped in Ali, unexpectedly, and I looked at my friend a bit embarrassed. I was thinking of slinking off; thinking these people have helped us enough already.

Brenna looked at him sternly, then she melted a little, her features softened. "C'mon," she said, "Let's get you away from here."

We tramped away from the trucks, over fields for a couple of hours. Brenna obviously knew where she was heading, knew how to keep out of the way of any people, out of sight. We passed over a few roads but this time didn't see our twin arteries south, the river and the railway. Ali and I had no idea where we were. There was no conversation until we entered the shade of a wood. Ali asked where we were going.

"You'll see," she said.

"Somewhere safe?"

Brenna laughed. "Safer."

"We appreciate your help," I said.

"Well, you'd do the same for us right?"

"Right." We would have. Without a doubt.

"What happened with the filth?" I asked. The word came out awkwardly; it wasn't really my style.

"The filth?" mocked Brenna in a hoity toity tone, sussing me straight out. "The filth placed one under arrest for threatening an officer of the law with a lethal weapon. One is required to attend a court of law next month but..." She grabbed a dead branch from a dying elm and used it to lash at the waist-high grass by the side of the crude path we were following. "They don't know what to do with me, do they? I'm too young for prison, and they know I'd run off if they chucked me in a borstal. I dunno. We might not even show in court. Arthur's worried, thinking of splitting the country. Maybe we'll go."

"Where to?"

"Don't know. Ireland maybe. France, Spain. Might go to London for a bit. Big site opening up Windsor way. Lots of apple picking nearby."

Spain. Our absurd plan from the nook was crystallising. I stopped suddenly and the party halted with me.

"We need to come too."

Brenna scoffed and looked us up and down incredulously. "No chance."

"What are we going to do then?"

"How the hell should I know? You killed a kid, you've got the law trailing after you like a pack of bloodthirsty hounds. Lord knows you've brought enough shit down on us already. In fact, screw you. Mind out for yourselves!" She threw the stick down with an air of finality and turned on her heel.

"No wait," I pleaded, "I'm sorry. We don't want to give you any more trouble, and we're grateful for the help you are giving us. Please. You were taking us somewhere safer?"

Brenna nodded slowly and eyed us warily. "Yep, helping you out because that's what our people do but don't push me, don't push us, or we'll snap and you'll get hurt." She looked intently at us. "Understand?"

We did. We nodded emphatically, but despite Brenna's firmness, real escape was opening up before our eyes. If these people can do it, we thought, then why can't we?

"So where we going?"

"You'll see."

We emerged from the wood and there were houses in the distance and we crossed a meadow, jumped a brook and picked our way through some wide, deserted streets with detached bungalows either side. We hit a path that skirted the back of a primary school, passing two women with pushchairs, and emerged on a busy road.

"Keep your head down," said Brenna, "Nearly there."

"Where are we?" said Ali.

"Wallingford. See that hedge?" She pointed at a scruffy bush at the mouth of a scrap of parkland. "Get behind there, where no one can see ya."

Ali and I obeyed and Squirrel reluctantly joined us, squatting sulkily with us out of sight. Brenna strode off purposefully and we sat uncomfortably on a patch of sparse grass and waited. Just when we thought she had abandoned us she re-emerged with a clinking plastic bag at her knee.

"What ya got?"

"Presents. Got any money?"

I wished we did. Then I remembered we had! "We have actually. What do you need?"

"Fiver?"

I reached into my filthy jeans and pulled out our bank, two filthy blue notes, one still folded and refolded into a triangular box, maybe by my mum. A wave of remorse for my theft and for the heart ache I was causing her surprised me. But I stayed resolute, the money was going to a good cause, I told myself, a donation to our life saver. I handed over the notes and Brenna took them with a shrug. Then we followed the road for a few hundred yards and turned into the mouth of an estate. Scruffy front gardens gave way to low red brick semis with tiny windows. A three storey block loomed and we made our way up to double meshed glass doors with six rows of two silver buttons beside it. Brenna pressed one, the number 240 etched beneath it and, after an interminable gap, a gruff strangely familiar voice barked out.

"Who is it?"

"Brenna Maguire."

And a buzzer sounded without further ceremony and we pushed our way into a dank functional hallway and mounted some concrete stairs. At the end of a grey disinfected corridor was the red brown door of flat 240, unremarkable in its scuffed anonymity. Brenna rapped at the door and it swung open. Wild Bill stood before us.

Eleven

THE RETURN TO ENGLAND

Bill waved us inside with gruff indifference. His filthy jeans, cowboy boots and wide brimmed Stetson were accompanied by a dandy red neckerchief. It stank and I fought back a gag as we followed Brenna inside: festering air, stale booze and some unidentifiable animal smell. I looked down. The floor was covered in straw! Mournful country and western music played from some hidden room.

"Close the door behind ya," he growled and looked Brenna up and down suspiciously. "Bring me something?" he demanded. Brenna thrust the plastic bag at Bill who seized it, pulled out two bottles of sherry and gave them a cursory examination.

"Good girl," he said, a bit more warmly now. "Brenna Maguire it is. And a game little girlie she is. Now how's my partner Arty Mac?"

"Not good Bill. You heard the site got turned over?"

"Heard that. Lawmen looking for some critters on the run. Heard that too." He looked intently at us.

"Arthur's thinking of quitting the country," said Brenna, changing the subject.

"Hitchin' up his wagon and heading out west?" laughed Bill. We were astonished at how dependent his mood was on the booze brought for him. "C'mon inside. You're old enough to take a drink now, ain't you?" He headed towards a living room with more straw on the floor. Belle was dozing in the corner and a dilapidated corduroy sofa and matching chair faced towards a window overlooking the outskirts of the town and the rolling hills and woods of South Oxfordshire. Improbably, Wild Bill had a home and we were in it. Brenna followed him in and we were about to follow our friend when Bill stopped us. "Hold ya horses!" he cried, "I can't remember inviting you little injuns in here."

Did Bill expect us to stand in the hall? Did he remember us from Oxford? I remembered him calling us injuns as we stared at his drinking gang by the church in Oxford and decided to formally introduce ourselves.

"Bill, my name is Richard. This is my friend Ali. Maybe you remember us?"

"Remember you?" At first he seemed amused that we should think such a thing possible but then he stopped and searched our faces, a sober scrutinising gaze passed over his features and for a second his face took on the countenance of an authority figure, a teacher or a doctor. "I do remember you. Scrabbling about by the railroad tracks. Throwing mud at the engines, wasn't it?"

I nodded. "We talked by the canal one day, you offered me some sherry." He was staring at me incredulously and so were the others but I couldn't stop myself now, it was flowing out of me. "You have friends in Oxford: Shanklin, Tim Physics, Mary. We thought we saw you were all dead but then we saw you again at Arthur's, where Brenna and Squirrel were living. Are they dead, Bill?" Ali elbowed me hard in the ribs and brought my little speech to a halt.

Bill stared long and hard at me. "Dead? Who?"

"Shanklin. Physics. Mary."

Bill searched my face for additional meaning. I realised he was searching for mockery, he couldn't believe I was spreaking in earnest. I met his gaze stolidly, after all we had seen it, hadn't we? We had seen them dead, I would have sworn it, and yet as Wild Bill stood before us unmistakably alive, my mind crowded with doubt. I cast my mind back to the four bodies in the trees. We didn't look at Bill as closely as the others it was true, but Shanklin, he wasn't breathing. And Physics? Well, Ali had said he saw his eyes open but I wasn't sure. To tell the truth, at this point I wasn't really sure of anything.

A wheeze broke cover from Bill's lips, squeezing out from his grizzled beard. Then he broke into a guffawing chuckle. "Ned Shanklin dead? No lad, no. Come on. Sit down."

He waved us onto one of the sofas and we took a seat: me, Ali and Brenna in a row on the sagging, filthy couch. Squirrel headed for Belle and crouched down to ruffle her sleeping neck affectionately. Bill disappeared into a back room somewhere and emerged carrying five chipped mugs and one of the bottles. He lined up the mugs, unscrewed the bottle top and prepared to slosh out the sherry.

"Small measures for us, Bill," said Brenna warily and Bill cackled dryly as he splashed a mouthful into the first four then filled his own up to the brim.

"What age are ya now?" he demanded of Brenna.

"14."

"Him?" said Bill, jerking a thumb at Squirrel, now lying full length alongside Belle kneading and rolling her belly like dough. The animal stretched in silent ecstasy, eyes closed and jaws wide.

"Only nine Bill," said Brenna gravely, "Too young for drink."

Bill nodded, a touch of sadness in his eyes. "Not for me, not when I was a young colt." He looked dreamily at the hills for a few seconds then picked up his mug and took a hefty swig. "Drink," he urged, "The little 'un's share's for the first to down their rounds." Ali and I smiled politely as we sipped the sickly, sweet, stinging liquor. It was not unpleasant. It had a sweet and numbing burr and a nauseous, heady after burn. Chugging it, even such a small measure, seemed a bad idea but Brenna finished hers without ceremony and casually poured

Squirrel's into her own mug. She pulled out her rollups and began to make one.

"You can make me one of them," said Bill. In explanation, he held out his quivering hands and grinned wryly. "Too many rattlesnake bites." He refilled his cup and contemplated his visitors. Efficiently, Brenna made Bill's rollup first and passes it to him. Bill lit up and, checking he had the attention of his audience, began.

"You were asking about Ned Shanklin. You thought you'd seen him dead and gone. What you saw was a dead man's sleep but not a dead man. Gentlemen of the road, we're obliged to sleep deep, to sleep out of reach of cold and cruelty. Deep and dark is where me, and people like me, sleep when we've drunk our fill. It protects us from the cold and from the harm of others. It'd take a barrel of whisky to put Ned's lights out for good and the same's true for the others. Same's true of me, especially true of me. Like I told you I've taken a drink since I was same age as the little 'un."

I glanced at Brenna. She knew if she wanted to keep Bill's mood hospitable she needed to keep him talking. She was calm, friendly and mildly enquiring. "Where was that Bill?"

"Ever since I arrived in London and before that as a matter of fact..." He tails off to rescue his cigarette and to replenish his cup. "Wanna hear a story do ya, kids? You've heard it before girlie, no doubt?"

"No Bill, not exactly."

"Well, you're going to hear it now, so I hope you're ready." He looked out again towards the hills and began. "Lots of people think I ain't a cowboy. Think the whole thing some kind of pantomime. Well I'm telling ya now, it's the truth. Born in Virginia, on a mountain cow farm."

"Where's Virginia, Bill?" asked Brenna. Her voice had deliberately taken on the enraptured hush of an enthralled child.

"Virginia? United States of America. Don't they teach you nothing at school these days?"

"We don't go to school, Bill."

"So you don't."

Bill looked suspiciously at Ali and me. "What about you silent Bobs? Partaking of a bit of schoolroom learning, are we?"

"Yeah, we're at school," I said shyly, not wanting to break the spell.

"Not with Arthur's tribe then? No. Fancy you are the two critters responsible for bringing down Arthur's house. Am I right?" We all sat dumbstruck, not knowing what to say. Squirrel paused from his quiet wrestling with Belle to see what the outcome of this standoff would be. But Bill just laughed. "Well, you know where Virginia is boys?"

"I do," I said, "America. On the Atlantic coast, capital Richmond, the mother of presidents."

"Schooled they are!" he exclaimed. "Well this little one is in any case. What he has done to pitch himself on the road I don't know." He looks at me hard with a scrutinising glare from beneath the brim of his hat then turns his stare on Ali. "Nor this little fella..."

"Should have known where Virginia is Bill," cut in Brenna.

"You should," exclaimed Bill, diverted again, "No schooling ain't an excuse. I never went to school much myself and never learnt much when I was there anyway. Still know the 52 states of America. I know that..."

"Tell us about that mountain cow farm," I interjected.

Brenna gave me daggers and Ali looked at me appalled but Bill warmed to the topic. "Yes, yes. My daddy owned that farm and he took it over from his daddy who got hold of it... well you can guess. It was a family business. And I was born into it in 1933, raised with mountain soil under my boots and the breeze from the Appalachians on my back. Though later I did go to school a little some and curbed my manners like my folks said to do, I only wanted one thing and that was to mind that farm like my daddy did."

Bill stared at us and we nodded politely and encouragingly. Bill's features softened a little, he tended to his smoke and refilled his drink, finding his rhythm. Like his canine companion, Squirrel had rolled over onto his back and the two cast a critical but respectful eye at the scene.

"I look back on my early days as pretty nice. But I soon realised that my mam wasn't as happy as me. Not for the first time here we had a woman that couldn't be satisfied. She was English yer see, a London girl. She came to New York in 1931 aboard an ocean liner. Part of the entertainment, a singer and a dancer, maybe even a good one. Good enough anyway for someone to pay her to roll back and forth across the ocean and entertain the folks making the crossing. I don't know how she met my pap. I don't know what brought him up to town, his farm and New York City are 300 miles apart but he made the journey and he met her and he persuaded her, or she persuaded him, to travel back with him and live with him on the farm with him and his daddy who was bed-bound. Pap was a silent type, always out in the fields or working in the barn. They were like chalk and cheese, him strong and silent; her all emotional most of the time. Like I said, she wasn't exactly happy and my memories then are often of her in tears although I recall her laughing also, she was always doing one or the other and never just sitting content doin' nuffin."

"One time mam gathered me up in her arms in the night and carried me out to pap's pick up. C'mon she said, we're goin'. Where we goin, mam? I asked. We're goin' home she says. It was just getting light. I remember that, the sky was full of bats. This here is my home, I said, but she just fell to crying as she took the wheel. She made it half a mile down the road before she wound up in a ditch. She couldn't drive ya see. Pap came and picked me up and took me back to bed, then he went back for her and done the same thing. Never saw him complain once, not even then. Anyways, after that we stayed but mam still blubbed all the time, saying she was made up for the stage, saying that she needed the grease paint, the lights, the crowds, saying she was dying out here on my daddy's farm. But still we stayed. Well now what do you think about that?"

With a shock we realised he was addressing us.

"You got mothers, ain't ya? Ya got mothers like that?" he demanded.

Ali and I shook our heads, but Brenna spoke up.

"I don't know, Bill. We don't see her do we?"

Bill looked sorry. "It's true, Bren, I forgot that. Your mother..." He gestured to include Squirrel too, "Yours mother was a fine woman. She was a little like mine maybe..." He drained the remainder of the first bottle of sherry and pointed suddenly and fiercely at Ali. "You. Get the other. Make it fast."

Ali scampered out and returned fast enough with the second bottle of sherry. He handed it to Bill and this time we didn't get offered any. Instead Bill filled his mug with gusto.

"Then one day my daddy got drafted. They were wanting strong men to fight in Europe and pap he was 30 years old, strong as an ox, disciplined and smart. They took him away. Myself and mam, we tried to mind the farm but really we didn't know the first thing. My granpap, pap's pap, he tried to help us but he was lame, struck down with a stroke, paralysed on one side. He could barely even talk but I listened to his mumbling and groaning, trying to pick up the wisdom that was there. I was determined to step into my daddy's shoes although I was only eight years old at the time. I teached myself to ride a horse and I tried to round up the animals, but I was too young. I couldn't do it. My mam, she would just sit and cry the whole time. Before my daddy left she said she had to go, she couldn't bear the life on the farm. She said that acting was in her blood, she said she had to feel the stage boards under her feet again. Now he was gone she said she missed old Abe, my pop, rotten. She said all she wanted was him safe and sound back from the war, back from France."

"The next thing that happened was that Abe's younger brother Frank showed up. Frank had gotten drafted too but he'd taken a bullet in the leg in Malta and he showed up on crutches to help mam. Well for a while things got better. Frank stabilised the farm and kept things on the straight and narrow but then, well, the worst' thing happened. Can you guess what that was?"

He was looking straight at me. "No," I said, "I can't."

"Guess." Everyone was looking at me. Bill was deadly serious, accusatory. He raised his voice a notch, a touch of fierceness was introduced. "C'mon, sonny, take a guess!"

"I don't know," I said desperately looking around me, "Frank went away again?"

"Oh, worse than that!"

"Frank took up with your mother," I said suddenly. It popped out; I even shocked myself by saying it.

There was a stunned silence. Ashen, Bill stared into my face. Brenna raised a palm. "He don't mean it, Bill. Don't blame him Bill."

Bill's face broke. He snorted and guffawed in appreciation. "Blame him?" he roared. "He's a smart little critter, this one! He knows the way of it." He picked up the sherry bottle and, abandoning the cup, took a generous slug. "Here, kid," he said, offering me the bottle, "Drink with me."

I took it and, trying to ignore the thought of Bill's spittle on the bottle's mouth, allowed the liquid to bounce against my lips. I sighed as if grateful and swallowed air.

"Actually pap died first," said Bill and began to chuckle darkly, ending with a wheeze and a coughing fit. When he had regained his composure, he rolled himself a cigarette, hands steady now, and continued. "Well who knows which way round it was? Pap came home in a box and ma took up with Frank? Or Frank took up with ma and then pap's coffin showed up? I simply couldn't tell ya. Either way pretty soon we were living like a kind of messed up family and I was growing up a farm child again but with Frank instead of Abe for a pap. And Frank was no Abe. Abe was kind and quiet, a tower of strength they called him, but Frank was more of a flitty fella, more of a wise guy, kinda guy who thinks he's cracking killer lines all the time when really he's just bugging the shit out of you. He couldn't run the farm like Abe could and he took to drinking too and drinking too much as well. Now you would say I'm a fine one to talk and you'd be right but fact is I've never run my mouth off, nor hit no women, nor hurt no one that didn't deserve it on account of drink. Brenna, you'll back me on that?"

Brenna looked up from her latest roll your own and nodded ardently.

"Virginia wasn't dry then, Prohibition got lifted in the state of Virginia in 1934. But by then, especially in the mountains there was a moonshine industry rivalling anything any serious liquor manufacturer coulda put together. Strong grog at basement rates and, well, Frank took to throwing the stuff back and soon he took to knocking ma about into the bargain. Oh, she wound him up, it's true. She'd say to him, you ain't nothing on Abe, you can't farm like Abe, you can't brand cattle like Abe, you ain't a man like Abe." Bill's eyes twinkled. "Now I didn't really know what she meant by that last remark at the time, but I do now, I do now." He chuckled, "Do you know, boys?" We laughed back politely but we were not sure that we did.

"Anyways, we saw out the war. Frank's drinking got worse and worse and soon he didn't have the strength to hit ma no more and didn't have the wherewithal to know when I was stealing the moonshine from right under his nose. Actually I got a taste for the drink right there on that farm with my ruined uncle and my unhappy mother and soon my dead granpappy too, so there's your answer right there, girl. My granpap he passed away the day before D-Day and the day after that it was my twelfth birthday. Well, by now I figured that the farm was my birthright and now granpap had passed away, there was only Frank standing in the way of the land that was rightfully mine. I knew all I had to do was keep feeding Frank the moonshine and he'd be out of the way too. Trouble was, same thing as before went on. Ma grabbed me in the night, she said, C'mon we're goin'. I said, not again mam, not this time. But she had this hold over me, like I couldn't say no and I guess I figured we'd only wind up in a ditch again but no, this time she done it! She drove through the night and we wound up in Lynchburg at daybreak. We ditched pap's old pick up and we got a train to New York City and then we stayed in some deadbeat downtown fleapit for a couple of days and then suddenly we was on a boat, sailing home to England!"

Bill had raised his voice to a crescendo at this point and rounded off the episode by theatrically draining the bottle. He looked down for a while after that and then looked up again, limp, defeated. "Least, she was sailing home, I didn't know where I was going. In fact I was leaving home." He looked around him, seemingly momentarily lost, then, as if catching sight of a light in a fog, fixed his gaze on me.
"You, injun with the dirty mind, there's whisky in the kitchen, side cupboard, top part, fetch it here."

I started up with a jolt and made my way down the filthy corridor where I found an even filthier kitchen, red stained worktops, kitchen cupboards with peeling paint like rancid cream, a corner festering with rotting rubbish. In the cupboard, sure enough, was an unopened bottle of whisky. I took hold of it and returned to the living room where Bill was still in full flow.

"...a city of filth. I saw it on the horizon and it looked like broken teeth in a rotting mouth. Liverpool. 1946. It was teaming with rain and the people looked ill, broken. We'd been through the war too in the US but we kept our dignity, folks in England looked washed up, grey, ghosts. I begged mam to get us back on a boat and get us home again, I didn't care about

Frank now, but she was radiant, smiling all the time, just you wait till we get home to London she said, just you wait. Well, I did wait. I held on as we sat on a filthy train heading south in more rain and cold and when we got to London... it was just as bad. Everything boarded up, rations, no smiles. Ah, the whisky!"

I presented Bill with the bottle. He took it gratefully and filled his cup. To our relief, he didn't offer us anything again. He was lost in the telling of his story.

"And mam found everyone was gone. She went to where she used to live, where she'd grown up, Shepherd's Bush, but the street was bombed out. Some folks roundabouts remembered her mam and pap and her twin baby brothers, but they didn't know where they had gone to. The war had picked up everybody and shook 'em up and thrown them all over. Mam didn't even recognise the place."

He paused to slug the whisky again, a little slower this time. I noticed Squirrel and Belle were asleep, sprawled luxuriously on the filthy floor.

"We took a poky little one room apartment in Notting Hill Gate and mam went out to work as a telephone receptionist in the Carreras cigarette factory. Only reason I knew that is 'cos she always had a few cartons of smokes in her pocket and she didn't mind me half-inching a few. See, she wasn't around much. In the day she went to work and in the evenings she was at some drama group or at least that's what she told me she was at. Anyways, I was kicking around the flat a lot on my lonesome and there wasn't much to do. Pretty soon, though, I discovered drinking in order to give my life some focus, drinking and the procurement of the said drink." Bill paused to chuckle to himself.

"I told you I had been raised on the moonshine back in Virginia. In London I got to realise that there was something missing in myself and soon I got to figure that that missing thing was the tang in the back of my throat and the burn in my stomach and the singing head that I got from drinking alcohol. Well, I couldn't get in the pubs and in any case I had no money so I had to be clever to get a drink. I stole a lot of money around Oxford Street and Regent Street, picked the purses of rich dames in Selfridges and Liberty's and conned tourists around the Palace with my American accent. Told them I was in London with my folks from Washington DC 'cos my dad was on a diplomatic visit, told them I had lost my folks, said if they could advance me an English pound I would be sure to return it by registered delivery. I very particularly noted their addresses but then I took their money and the dames' purse money and went to the shops in Notting Hill and Edgeware Road where you could buy bottled ale and cider off the shelf. Mostly I got away with saying it was for my pap. I scribbled a note saying very formal like from him that on account of his war wound he was bed bound and could his good son be entrusted to deliver something of a little comfort to a war hero? And the like. But otherwise well I just hung around until a likely looking character slid by, then I'd bribe him to do my booze buying for me. Younger than you now, kids, and drinking myself to oblivion ever night."

Bill's voice rose suddenly to a bark and we all looked up at him terrified. "So when you look at me you see a man made of the drink, made out of hardship, made out of suffering but don't..." His voice dropped down to a whisper again. "Don't ever doubt my sincerity."

Now he paused. He looked directly at us, his eyes watery with booze or tears I was not sure, and for a second I could see the young Bill as he was back then in the war years, a fresh faced ruffian with a Yankee drawl and a gut full of determination; and all the absurd cowboy talk made sense.

"I started off telling you about the deep sleep about how it protects me and people like me from the world," Bill said wearily. He looked spent now, worn out from the drinking and the telling of his tale. I wanted to know more now but we were not going to get anything else. Bill was finished. There was no neat ending to his tale. He rocked back a little where he was sitting right on the beaten up old sofa; we watched in astonishment as he closed his dilapidated eyes and immediately started to snore heartily.

Brenna shrugged and got to her feet. She looked briefly and tenderly at the slumbering Squirrel and headed for the door.

"Where you going?" said Ali.

"Spare room down the hall, cleanest place." She disappeared briefly and returned with a couple of blankets that didn't look too unhygienic. She lay one carefully on top of her sleeping brother and tucked it underneath him then threw one casually at me. "This will keep you warm," she said.

Then she turned briskly to Ali, "Well murder boy, looks like there's only room for Rich on that sofa so you're in with me."

I didn't know if Ali was as shocked as I was. I guessed he was as no one moved straight away. If there was something between them, I had not noticed it before. A thundering snore from Bill broke the silence.

"Well, are you coming or not?" said Brenna tartly and, to my astonishment, Ali shrugged and got up to leave with Brenna.

It had been a few nights since I had slept on anything soft so after they left and I heard a door shut softly closed, I lay back on the sofa and, despite the fetid odours and Bill's disturbing rasp, marvelled at the comfort. Belle snuffled and scratched and Bill let loose another monster snore but still sleep was fast advancing on me. Fourth night away: one in the nook, one in the hide, one in a bush and now this, curled up in Bill's hovel. But it was warm and safe and Ali and I had learnt how to eke out an existence from nothing. Who would have given us, Blake's terrified little charges, any chance as we had picked our way out of town? Now we were men of the road and like men of the road do, Ali had got with a girl. I felt a curious mixture of bewilderment, revulsion and jealousy about that but I couldn't process those emotions then. And soon my exhaustion dragged me into the grips of a dark, impenetrable sleep.

Twelve
KILLED A BOY

Hot light started turning my eyelids pink. Strong and potent, it tugged me up from the depths of sleep. I opened my eyes and the sickly sunshine made me swoon and sneeze. Belle was panting gently in front of me, tongue lolling expectantly, Squirrel stared mournfully out at the hills, looking for the first time like a lost and neglected child. Bill was missing from his chair. As I lay on his filthy couch, I remembered Ali and Brenna's disappearance with a sharp pang something like jealousy. Everything had changed again, the latest turn in a kaleidoscope of upheaval: Blake was dead, Wild Bill alive, and my friend was in bed with a traveller girl.

"Morning," I offered Squirrel, "how did you sleep?"

Squirrel turned and scowled but then seemed to relent. His eyes pleaded a little, and he rubbed his stomach yearningly.

"Hungry?" I asked. I considered Bill's flat and concluded we were unlikely to find any food in the squalor. I smelt piss, strong, acidic, and sat up, back suddenly stiff, head throbbing. The sherry had parched me out and I needed a drink of water. I got gingerly to my feet and retraced last night's steps to the putrid kitchen. Passing an ajar bedroom door, I heard a grunt and a moan. It was Bill, obviously taken to his bed in the night. I made sure I stayed as quiet as possible as I entered the kitchen and, after sloshing a little tap water around one of the chipped mugs to wash it out, filled one up for a drink. Ok, I told myself, the place stank but at least, I thought, we were safe here. It was a stopping off point in our flight that had become an addiction, something we were determined to see out to the end, whatever that end might have been. Well, I thought as I gingerly sipped at the water, at least we were in it together. What the future might hold if Brenna was now Ali's girlfriend I could not say. I shrugged to myself and, as quietly as I could, took a root around for something to eat. There was next to nothing: instant coffee, more whiskey, a few stale crackers. I did find a stash of dog food cans and loaded a filthy red plastic bowl for Belle and she sauntered in and gratefully began to lap it up.

I brought a few of the crackers through to Squirrel, sat down with my chipped mug and waited for Ali to get up. I was hungry again but easy in the knowledge that food would arrive soon, like it always had. We had no money left after giving the last to Brenna but we had lived without spending money for five nights, save a couple of quid in a corner shop when we were wet behind the ears and a tenner for last night's host's refreshment. We were men now, I told myself, gentlemen of the road, wily and willing to slip the law and live off our wits. But would Brenna want to take my friend away now? I felt a stab of anger. She couldn't. She had no right. I wished then that I was Blake's killer. Then I would have had to stay on the road.

"Rich." Ali appeared. He looked a little sheepish but rested, his hair tousled, his eyes still bleary with sleep.

"Hey," I said, trying to keep any resentment out of my voice.

Squirrel smiled. Brenna was at the door too, coat on, ready to leave. From behind her a titanic rasp of snoring broke out from Bill.

"We're going back to site," she said to Squirrel, who obediently took his place at her side. "Look," she said to Ali, "it's goodbye now. We can't see you again for a long time, can't help you again." Why hadn't she told him all this in private? I wondered and decided it must have been for my benefit too; she wanted us both to hear. Sure enough, then she held out her hands to include the two of us. "I like you, both of you, and I wish you well, sounds like the kid you stuck had it coming to him, but we can't help you no more. You can shelter here for a while if you can stand Bill and all his crap. Up to you. Fair enough either way."

"No, we're going too," said Ali, a touch of defiance in his voice. "We're going to find my dad."

Brenna shrugged and they left. Ali and I sat down side by side on Bill's sofa. Belle looked at us mournfully. Ali stared out at the hills. He was thinking and I gave him time to do it but I wanted to break the spell Brenna had cast on him and I didn't know how to. Eventually we heard Bill stumbling around and cursing and shortly afterwards he appeared in the doorway. He looked at us severely, all the bonhomie of the previous night gone. It was the first time I had seen him without his Stetson and, in the clear light of morning he truly looked the drunken wreck in his late forties that he was. With the Stetson on, his raven locks hung neatly and straggle of beard at his chin lent him a tough sheen of vigour but, without the hat, I could see the thinning of his hair. His face looked paler too and more obviously marked by the damage of the drink, his skin puffy and irritated; his eyes watery. His hands visibly ticked and quivered. I knew we had to be away from this man and his uneasy hospitality.

"Well, boys," he said quietly, "on the run, eh?"

"Yes," I said, "and we're grateful for your hospitality last night but we should be off..."

"Off? Off to where?"

"Reading," cut in Ali. "My dad's there."

Wild Bill wheeled round to regard Ali. He looked carefully at my friend and his demeanour softened a little. "What ya do kid?" he asked gently.

"Killed a boy."

Bill looked interested. "He deserve it?

"Yeah."

"I killed a boy once too, y'know. Well he deserved it all right. And you know what else? I got away with it too." We looked in astonishment at the pathetic figure in front of us. His confession was deeply disturbing, we were getting dragged into a world of irredeemable souls, the kingdom of the damned. "If you want to," he said eventually, "you can ride a train to Reading out of Didcot. Best to ride a taxi cab to the station. You'll need some money too." He trailed off as if lost in his thoughts then suddenly looked at us intently. "I'm going to offer you some advice though, kid," he said to Ali. "Seeking out your pa, it's a natural thing to do but I'm telling you it's the worst thing too. If you wanna stay free, you gotta break off any tie you got, you gotta give them nothing to go on, you gotta start again. And a pa's the strongest link you got. They're going to be expecting that you go running to him and be waiting there for you."

Ali nodded slowly if not in agreement then in respect for the point. "Who you kill, Mister?" he asked gently.

"I'll tell ya," said Bill, "But I'm going out for supplies first. I don't like getting out without a drink to clear my head and I was going to send you two but I figure that, in the circumstances, it's better I go myself."

And so we waited awkwardly in Bill's filthy hovel for his return, sitting in glum silence. The telepathy between me and Ali was scrambled. Neither of us could find words for each other. After a little while, Belle pleaded with me again and, grateful for an excuse to leave the lounge, I got up, went back to the kitchen and gave her the remainder of the tin I had started earlier. Then I returned to Ali, taking my place beside him in the wreckage of Wild Bill's broken existence, wondering if I belonged here at all anymore. I wished I could ask Ali about Brenna or that he would mention it; it was the great unspoken stumbling block between us. But neither of us brought it up.

Bill returned whistling good humouredly and, with the Stetson returned to his crown, looked his normal self once more. His hands were full: local and national newspapers, tobacco, sherry, whisky (he had taken a nip to steady himself) and beer, money, a loaf of bread, some peanut butter, a pot of jam and more instant coffee. Waving us into our seats he produced perfectly drinkable coffee heavily laced with sugar and possibly a jolt of whisky and two gigantic slabs of bread, peanut butter and jam to go with it.

"Look for yourselves, boys," he said, thrusting the papers in our direction, "take a look in the news." We did and were almost disappointed to find nothing in the *Daily Mirror*, nothing in the *Wallingford Herald* and nothing in the *Oxford Times*.

That's it then: we were forgotten, even Blake's murder was yesterday's news. Bill threw two ten pound notes down in front of us. "Money for a cab and a train. Walk back to the main road, turn right. There's a taxi rank there." He looked intently at Ali. "And remember, seeing your father is a mistake." Ali nodded but I knew we would still try to find him. We had always said we would do that. Bill stared impassively at us, one eyebrow raised slightly. I realised he was waiting for us to leave.

One more thing. "You were going to tell us about the man you killed, Mr Bill," I reminded him.

A spasm of annoyance crossed his brow. Then he thought better of it. "Murder? Murder in the first?" he drawled dryly. "Wanna hear another tale, do you?" He unscrewed the cap on the whisky bottle slowly and took a big pull. Then, he put it to one side, replaced the cap carefully and snapped open a tin of beer. "Take the whisky away from me, son," he said, suddenly grave as he handed me the bottle.

I left the bottle in the kitchen and when I got back he had

117

started telling Ali his murder story. Feeling a little annoyed at not being included from the start, I took my place awkwardly beside my friend.

"... I just got tired of all the running around looking for drink and sitting in that freezing apartment waiting for ma to never show. I took off along the river heading west. I walked for the whole day and when evening fell I found a little shelter in the gardens of Hampton Court and laid my head down on the bench. It was a warm evening, same time a year as now I guess and I soon dropped off. But then I got rudely awakened with a torch beam in my eye and hostile shouting and there was some drunken fools standing afore me. I tried saying leave me alone, I'd move along or whatever but they're not listening to reason. Next thing I know, one of thems landed a mighty blow to my head. I rolled off the bench and onto the ground and the boots come flying in and then I managed to get to my feet and I lumped one of them and then took off running. Well you might not think it now but I could run good in my day..."

Ali and I nodded eagerly. Bill took a long, deep sip of his beer. He looked incredulously at the can, as if he had been cheated by what was inside, then carried on.

"Well in trying to get away I ran into the maze, and the crew came hollering and shouting after me. I was panicked and I knew they'd soon have me cornered and then I tripped and my hands clasped round a bit of rock making up the path edge, a fistful of flint, a caveman's weapon." Bill broke off and began to roll a cigarette. "You'll know, the toll on a man's heart. It don't go away. They meant to kick the living daylights out of me, fancied raining some damage down on a hobo and have no one to answer to for it. I ran up behind one of them and I smashed his head in. Never forgot it. I could feel his whole skull give way under my fist. Anyways, I saw the story on a newspaper board the next day so I knew what it was. Murder."

Suddenly he looked spooked, gripped in a horrific recollection buried thirty years away. He fixed his gaze on Ali. "It will stay with you for life boy. Either way you'll pay for it in your soul but it's up to you if you wanna pay for it with your time too. I never have."

He stared deep into Ali's eyes. "Time to run boy," he murmured, "And not look back." We stared at him expectantly but he was not letting anything else out. He held our stare hard and sent it straight back. We just grabbed the notes and left.

Thirteen

MR. STEVEN JOHNSTON

The weather finally broke at Reading: a flash of lightening, crescendo of thunder and then a splatter of rain at the window. Rain: it was a miracle after four dry arid weeks. Slumped in grim silence in our train seats, we watched the city's urban sprawl unfold outside the carriage window. The telepathic understanding that had kept us safe and fighting for freedom was still missing. Ali stared out at the darkening rooftops. I knew it was Brenna that had broken our rhythm, and I imagined that was what he was thinking about. But I couldn't ask him; somehow we had lost the ability to talk.

"Rain," I said.

Ali nodded. I was hoping he might open up, but he just carried on staring vacantly out. Another angry sprawl lashed at the window and with it I felt a noticeable loss of pressure in the carriage; a draft of cold air arrived at our elbows. I gave up trying to engage my sulky friend and stared out of the window too.

As we stepped from the train, it was pouring. The grey aluminium canopy protecting the platform rattled like a snare drum and, through a mist of condensation and cigarette smoke, we could see floods gushing down the flanks of the train on the opposite platform. I stopped, taking in the army of commuters shaking and folding their umbrellas. To my surprise, Ali stopped too. At least he noticed I was here, I thought. But in the crowd his presence was melting away, as if he were just another stranger. The crowds were oppressive; it felt like I hadn't seen so many people in years; ugly, milling faces rushing onto trains. The force of the wild was still with us and I observed the crowd as if from a distance, as if looking at an ant's nest. I looked across the bubble at Ali, tried a wry smile and was surprised to get one back. Cheered, I pointed towards an exit where a fat little ticket inspector barely looked at our tickets. No one cared and that was good and that was bad. It had been the same on the train and before that in the taxi in Wallingford. We were forgotten. The living dead.

Outside the station we stood in front of the downpour. The commuters arriving behind us performed the opposite of those leaving, like video tape scrolled backwards, thrusting their umbrellas into the sky as they headed out into the wet, leaving us standing vacantly in our stale clothes. We were yesterday's news. Or more exactly yesterday's minor story on page seven of a distant local rag. I felt a chill, enough to make me shiver. And with it came the recognition that life would be harder on the run in the cold and the wet. We pulled the collars of our jackets around our necks but knew it was useless; we would be wet through in minutes when we walked out into this rain.

"So how do we get to your dad's?"

Ali looked a bit disturbed by the question.

I need to ask my dad, he said. My dad will know what to do.

That logic had carried us across woods and meadows, stayed with us as we slept in hedgerows and travellers' camps. Now we were about to find out: would Ali's dad really be able to help us?

Wild Bill's words came floating back too.

Seeking out your pa it's a natural thing to do but I'm telling you it's the worst thing too. If you wanna stay free, you gotta break off any ties you got, you gotta give them nothing to go on, you gotta start again. And a pa's the strongest link you got. They're going to be expecting that you go running to him and be waiting there for you.

"He lives at Flat 2, 46 Kirkwood Drive. Mr Steven Johnston," said Ali mechanically.

I glanced sideways at my friend. He was as lost in thought as I was. I nodded in recognition and looked carefully at the offices and the cars churning past the station's entrance, their wheels sending the puddles flying onto the pavements. The rain had nearly stopped, it was just a heavy shower. A slither of sunshine broke through the bank of cloud in the eastern sky.

"Know how to get there?"

Ali shook his head. I decided to take control. A young woman pushing a pram with jet black hair scraped back from a thin pale face passed us. "Excuse me," I said. She looked at us suspiciously as I gave her Ali's dad's address and shook her head. But after several more attempts we found someone who knew where it was. "Kirkwood Drive?" said a young man in blue overalls with an open friendly face. "I know it, down Earley way."

"Is it far to walk?" asked Ali.

He looked at us doubtfully. "You could walk it." He gave us brief directions.

We tramped out of the city centre and walked along the edge of a park in the shade of some oaks with a busy road thundering eastwards on our left. We were silent, lost in our own doubts and dreams. Day six on the road and we were reaching a crescendo. Ali's dad would turn us in surely. I looked around with regret. Our adventure was surely nearly over. Soon our world would be ruled by adults again.

We crossed another busy road and headed down a road with a lot of Indian restaurants and newsagents. Plenty of the people had black and Asian faces and most of those that didn't were young and scruffy with long hair or dyed punk styles. We attempted to check our progress by asking a dreadlocked man sitting outside a West Indian grocer's about Kirkwood Drive.

He looked contemptuously at us and barked something un-intelligible in patois and we fled in terror. A group of young men, sporting mutton chop sideburns who looked tough but spoke in surprisingly soft gentle voices hadn't heard of Kirk-wood Drive. But they seemed keen to help and led us to an A to Z map in a busy newsagents.

Following the map's directions, we watched the ramshack-le high street dissolve into more anonymous suburban ter-races, lace curtained windows shielding the lives within from intrusion. I was lost in thought, dazed from lack of sleep and confusion. And then suddenly I noticed I was walking alone and turned around to see Ali 50 yards behind me, stopped dead in his tracks. Ahead of us was a large impersonal pub surrounded by a large car park. It was full of battered build-ers' vans with tabloid newspapers on dashes and piles of lad-ders and overalls piled up against rear windows. A shaven headed youth with a cigarette hanging from his mouth was putting clean ashtrays out on tables arranged in the sun. It was as if the downpour never happened: another hot day. A group of tough looking young men in white vests and jeans, pints of stout in hand, were about to sit down. But I guessed that the reason Ali had stopped was the presence of a smaller, pallid man with fine, pinched features and greying temples, in a grey shirt and a thin navy tie under a brown leather bomber jacket. He glanced briefly up the street before turning away and purposefully entering the pub.

I walked back to Ali who grabbed my arm and led me away from the pub and the main road up a side street of terraces with tidy front gardens. We ducked into a small deserted chil-dren's play park. Ali sat down heavily on a bench.

"What is it?" I asked. But I already knew.

"That was him. My dad."

"He wouldn't have known it was you..."

"I've seen him now. And that's enough. He can't help us."

"He didn't expect to see you. He didn't know you because..."

"Because he doesn't know me. He doesn't know me."

"No." I sat down next to Ali who was fretfully running the sole of one of his worn trainers over a small round stone. "No, Ali. It's not fair. It's not fair on him and it's not fair on you. He can't be blamed. He didn't expect to see you, so he didn't see you." Ali looked up warily and I sensed a breakthrough.

"It's like if you saw Lorimer," I said, thinking of the Leeds United collage on Ali's bedroom wall, "Lorimer, kicking a ball about right over there." I pointed towards a small patch of tired mud and scrubby grass at the edge of the swings. "You wouldn't believe it was him. It's too unbelievable. I don't know. The mind plays tricks." I faltered as I grappled for the right words to express this idea.

Ali got up and kicked the stone with all his might at the swing frame. It ricocheted alarmingly off an upright with a sharp resounding ping. Despite himself, he couldn't suppress a wry half grin.

"He looked at you," I said again, "right at you. But well... the mind plays tricks."

Ali looked at me kindly. "Thanks, Rich. You really are a mate and I know what you're saying but it's not that. I know people don't recognise each other sometimes, even when they're family. It's not that. It's just, I know now. He can't help me."

He sat down beside me again and we brooded for a while. A young mother arrived with two noisy boys who clambered on the climbing frame screaming the word 'takedown' at one another. The mother looked suspiciously at us; we had taken the only seating in the park and didn't have much business being there in any case. But we didn't move.

"Well, what are we going to do then?" I said eventually. Nothing came back. He stared at his feet. "Is Brenna your girlfriend?" Too late. It had slipped out. At least it got his attention.

"What?"

"Well, is she?"

"No..." But there was uncertainty in his voice. I hoped he would open up then but he seemed as confused as I was. Then he took a deep breath and turned towards me. I grinned: he was ready to tell me it didn't matter, Brenna, his dad, none of it. We are a team, he would say, we have come too far to stop now.

"Rich, you should go home."

My throat tightened, tears welled up. "No."

"Yes. You're innocent."

"So are you!"

"No."

"Well, I won't go home," I wanted to be guilty too, I wanted to stay on the run with my friend. Too much had passed between us for me to quit.

"You're a mate," he said gently.

"I know." I wanted everything to go back to how it was before but I knew it was impossible. Something had changed in my friend. He looked resigned, a little beaten. "Well, where are we going next?" I added eventually.

"We need to find work," said Ali, "And we need to stay out of the way of the law."

"Maybe the travellers?"

"Maybe." But Ali looked doubtful. Evidently whatever had passed between him and Brenna had drawn a line under further contact.

"Spain?"

Ali smiled wearily. That was a pipe dream; we both knew that now. Then he looked at me carefully: he had thought of something.

"Rich, maybe you were right about my dad." That's the spirit, I thought. That's my friend. I felt vindicated, an equal whose views were respected rather than a kid whom Ali had outgrown. I nodded earnestly. "I need to try again," he continued, "to be sure. But I can't go in there and face him. Will you... go in there... the pub... and find him?"

"Go in the pub?"

"Yes. Please."

"Now?"

"Yes."

Of course: to prove my commitment to the cause, if nothing else. But I knew it wouldn't work, I could see that just by looking at Mr Steven Johnston that telling him about Ali would bring us nothing but trouble. He wouldn't help his son; the only person who could help him was me and himself, a winning team. But I would try. I would show Ali how committed I was to our cause. What he needed now, I thought, was a demonstration of my faith. And I would give him that. Without another word I got to my feet and headed out of the park back towards the pub, leaving Ali at the bench.

Even in the 20 minutes or so Ali and I had been in conference at the play park, numbers had grown significantly in the pub. The parking spaces were nearly full and the benches outside heaved with men in paint splattered overalls or T-shirts and jeans. They glanced at me, momentarily diverted from their conversations, but as I approached the door, they returned to their cigarettes and sun soaked banter. I walked into near darkness: a beer soaked cave reeking of stale fag smoke. A fruit machine rattled and blinked as another idle painter with dungarees bunched around his waist pummelled it. Groups of men gathered around jugs of bitter and the racing papers and ahead, past dark wood panelling and empty tables, the dim lights of a garish bar shrouded in a film of yellow nicotine beckoned me. I could see no sign of the man we had glimpsed earlier.

Behind the bar a woman in a black dress, with platinum locks piled over a heavily made up face and dangerous looking pink pointed nails, eyed me suspiciously. Behind her an elder man was serving a group of men at the bar.

"Yes, love?" she said flatly. I wasn't sure if she expected me to order a drink.

"I'm looking for someone."

"Oh yeah." She didn't seem surprised. Maybe a son seeking an errant father was a regular occurrence around there. "Who would that be then?"

"Mr Steven Johnston," I said hesitantly. "He came in here a little while ago."

"Plenty of people came in here a little while ago," broke in the man behind the bar dryly. He had a puffy, baggy face and cruel hooded eyes.

"Mr Johnston? Steven Johnston?" muttered the woman and then shouted out to the dozen or so souls gathered in the pub, "Anyone know a Steven Johnston?" The parties gathered around tables and the bar mumbled uncertainly to themselves.

"You mean Steve? You looking for Steve?" A small man with a check shirt, leathery sun tanned skin and snow white curls stepped forward.

"Oh Steve," said the woman. "He's looking for Steve." She pointed in my direction.

"He's got a leather jacket," I said, "grey hair, a bit." I trailed off. My description wasn't top notch and they were looking at me with curiosity and increasing suspicion.

"Steve's gone off for a bit," said the man in the check shirt evenly. "If it is Steve you want. What do you want with him anyway?"

I had not considered that I would need to make a decision or explain myself and it suddenly occurred to me that I needed to be careful about what I said too. News of our crime and escape was relatively recent after all and might well be known about by the people in this pub. I felt panic rise in my chest, like the suffocating feeling Ali and I felt when we were trapped under water hiding from the police boat. I tried to stay calm, keep close to the truth, tried to keep my voice as slow and steady as possible.

"I'm a friend of his son."

"Is everything all right?" said the woman behind the bar. She was looking at me with concern now, with great gentle bovine eyes. I felt the need to run again soon. Fight or flight.

Flight.

"Hang on," interrupted the man with the hooded eyes, "You're not the runaways are you?"

Flight.

"Christ!" said the man with the checked shirt. "Steve's boy!"

I charged for the door, dimly aware of the sound of bar stools hitting the floor: they were after me. I belted across the car park and I heard the hue and cry begin as the burly builders left their pints, mobilised into a pursuing force. Now it really was over. Now things would change: there had been a sighting at last.

Police seeking the whereabouts of   the escaped teenage killers Richard   Turner and Alistair Johnston have reported a sighting at a public   house in Reading. One of the boys,   Richard Turner....

I ran straight across the road. A car bonnet howled close and there was a screech of tyres, a trail of oaths let loose. But I was already up the street with the neat terraces. I needed to arrive at the play park and get Ali before we were both caught. Impossible maybe but I needed to try. I would call his name at the gate. Together we would try and evade capture again, even if it was our last desperate act as criminals on the run.

Here. The gate.

Ali was not there.

I glanced back. Half a dozen burly men were charging up the road. Ali was not there. Fight or flight. Run. Ali was not there. I ran and ran. Like when Macaulay chased me but faster and uphill. Through a stitch and out the other side. The terraces became an estate; there were several choices of direction. I took the roads that led uphill, desperately hoping not to run into a cul-de-sac, knowing my young fresh lungs and legs had the men beat. Still faster, finding the energy from somewhere, not sure where. Ali was gone. His asking me to go into the pub had been a trick. *Rich, you should go home.* Fury rose in my chest. I would not go home! And I would outrun my pursuers. A footpath to my left and I stole a glance behind me. The roads behind me were empty but they would be calling the police. And now they had a sighting; now they could tighten the net. The path was flanked on both sides by the red brick sides of houses, then I was running past gardens and the back of some allotments. Familiar territory and no surprise when a railway embankment rose up before me. The path passed underneath a concrete arch but I didn't hesitate. I was racing up the sides of the embankment, heading for the dense hawthorn bushes at the tracks' side. Home territory: back to the nook, or a nook. I rolled into the foliage, letting the damp cool of the leaves fold around me.

Fourteen

THE HALL OF MIRRORS

So there I was, alone again. Ali had gone on without me. But at least, I told myself, I'm at home by the tracks again, in an impenetrable nook once more. A train was arriving, its clamour building. I heard the tracks buzz and creak, heard the wind whistle and then braced myself as the magnificent chunk of roaring steel passed a few feet from my head. The comfort and familiarity of the sound was troubling. Maybe I could only hear the world as it was while the rush of metal and the roar of diesel blocked everything else out. The noise subsided and I listened again for the shouts and sirens of pursuers. Nothing. Maybe, I thought, they had Ali. I pictured him cuffed, a uniformed officer with his hand on his head as he was pushed into a jammy dodger.

No. I knew they had not caught my friend. And I knew they wouldn't. I would find him first.

I lay in that hawthorn bush until the early evening, thinking and listening out for the police. Dozens of trains passed and, as I become accustomed to the havoc they wreaked on my resting place, I slowly began to pick out the regularity of their visits: four an hour, whistling by in groups of two, a five minute gap between each pair then a longer hiatus of around 25 minutes. I knew the longer I remained undiscovered the less focused the hunt would become. I was absolutely sure too that, like me, Ali had evaded capture. We were too clever for them, physically too small, too anonymous and too desperate. The question then was not would I find Ali but how would I find Ali? I considered first his motives for ditching me and concluded they were entirely honourable. My friend had assumed all responsibility for Blake's death and wanted to save me from the fugitive's life he saw as his only option. However, I knew that when I found him he would be grateful for my companionship and resourcefulness and would welcome me back. By abandoning me, I reasoned, Ali was actually testing my commitment to the cause, his cause, the right to live a life without paying for a forced mistake. Both of us assumed the penalty would be huge: courts, prison, and borstal, the life-long brand of 'criminal' and 'disturbed child' always with us. Maybe we were wrong about that, I thought, as I manoeuvred my pack so it rested behind my head wedged against a heavy root, but it was too late in any case: we had run and found the momentum of flight and now as each rootless day passed we were finding it harder and harder to stop.

I knew Ali felt the same. I had known him as a close, best friend for years and had lived by his side for a week. I knew him well as anyone and I resolved to try as best I could to think like he would. Where would he go? He said he needed to work and he needed to stay out of the way of the law. Neither would be easy for a 14 year old boy on the run. I considered options: farm work of some sort, seasonal fruit or vegetable picking maybe, or something under the wing of an adult. Wild Bill? Maybe Ali would go back to him in desperation, I thought, but he wouldn't be desperate yet. He would want to try striking out on his own first. Like Wild Bill himself said, if you want to stay free you have to break off every tie you've got. Brenna? She had made her position clear at Bill's: she wanted no more to do with either of us. But what if that was a smokescreen, a performance calculated to fool me into thinking they wouldn't meet again? A plot hatched in bed? I felt the whiplash of betrayal, a wounding sting, but then my reasoning returned. Even if Brenna's declaration was an act, she couldn't shelter Ali on site; it would be too dangerous and anyway Arthur wouldn't stand for it. And she already had Squirrel to look after.

Hours passed. I watched the sunlight thrown across the rails recede slowly. Out of the quickening evening, an express train shattered the peace, exploding past on the track and as it broke and rattled the air around me, I reached a sudden understanding: Ali would follow the river. It had helped us so far, given us life and shelter and brought us food and friends. Ali would not want to return towards Oxford and would want to grow outwards and away from the scene of the crime. He couldn't wait around for Brenna and she couldn't help him anyway, I reasoned. Of course, I realised, the river Thames led to London, to anonymity and disappearance, maybe even it could be the gateway to the flight abroad Ali mentioned. Spain. America. Well why not? Yes, Ali would follow the river and he would be skirting its path right now although, like me, he had more likely gone to ground for a few hours. I smiled to myself.

Another train followed five minutes later and I had a plan. Once the train passed I paused to listen. All quiet. A sticking window was forced shut some way away and a car ambled through the estate, a few distant voices from the allotments. Nice and quiet. Time to go. I climbed down the elevated mound of earth that carried the railway out of town, through the clumped bush and bramble and on to the same path I used to get away from the men in the pub. No one was there. A few bent backs in the allotment tending to patches but they weren't looking at me. I set off under the bridge, in a direction I took to be south easterly, away from the setting sun and towards where I imagined the river would be waiting to carry me away from this city towards my reunion with Ali.

A young man on a bike approached. He had fishing tackle stacked and piled across the rack at the back of his bike. I checked my stride but he just nodded at me evenly, not surprised or bothered by me, and I smiled at my return to anonymity. It only occurred to me once he had passed that the fishing tackle meant the river was near. I felt lucky, alive and alert: a true survivor.

Sure enough, the football pitches gave way to a series of lanes that in turn dissolved into quiet rows of terraced houses. Finally, I made my way through a network of tidy red cottages and there is was: the Thames, opening up before me. It had swollen into a formidable tract of fast flowing water, maybe 50 yards across. I paused to take in the majesty of the water and the hopes that I carried with it. It had grown with us: broadened and deepened as we had learnt to survive alone. But at that point I was alone beside it and I felt a pang of irritation with my friend. He had left me in the dark to fend for myself. Maybe, I thought, he thought I would limp home alone like a wounded dog. No chance. I would find him and then he would regret giving me the slip. He would realise that he couldn't exist without me.

I scanned both sides of the riverbank carefully for Ali. There were a few people about - several dog walkers grimly steered their charges home and a couple or two wandered hand in hand towards a row of terraces giving out onto the waterfront – but there was no sign of my friend. In front of the houses, the sickly orange streetlights emphasised the gathering blackness at the terraces' end and it was towards this dark that I headed. I took the unlit river path in the direction the water flowed, suppressing any anxiety and telling myself that this was how I would find Ali and that, as it always had before, things would turn out OK.

I followed the path for a mile or two as it skirted the river, sometimes flanked on my right by the sinister blackness of woodland, sometimes by a road and sometimes by smart river front houses. Behind me, the sky was shot with an afterthought of lurid pink, the finale to an unsettled day. But I noticed the dark was falling earlier: summer was coming to an end. Eventually the river path gave way to a scrubby common ringed by the anonymous lights of unremarkable semi-detached houses set back beyond a busy road. There was a silent giant dome, a clutch of smaller tents and rakish clawing metal limbs silhouetted in the fading light. It was a travelling funfair, partly assembled, uninhabited and black and sullen in the gathering dark.

I looked around for Ali again. I knew somehow he had been there. Maybe even he was there now. I thought of the boys who worked the rides, stepping lazily off the backs of moving dodgems and manning the fronts of rides with cloth money sacks at their waists. Could Ali become one of these boys? Who knows? Would he have thought of it? Yes. My closeness to Ali would lead me to him; my knowledge of his fugitive logic and resilience would allow me to find him, eventually. Before the police? Certainly. But before Macaulay? Of that I was not sure. I have something the police don't, he had said, I trust my instincts. Their search was all procedure, he had said, he worked on instinct. Did he really, I wondered. Or was the whole thing a bluff? The lunatic idea of calling him up emerged. I could test his claim that he only wants to help us, I thought. No. I knew I would be an idiot decision but I hadn't forgotten his number either.

Then I saw the clutch of trucks and caravans clustered in a corner of the common. This was where the people who ran the fair were camped up. All was quiet there but the lights in most of the caravans showed there were people inside. They would be a different community from Arthur's brigade of tough merrymakers, I reasoned, but similar in some ways: people of the road, proudly living apart from normal life. I resolved to speak to them in the morning. If Ali wasn't inside one of the caravans I was sure they would have seen him. I knew I was on the right track, thinking as my fellow fugitive did.

But right then I needed somewhere to rest until morning and the tents I saw first, the ones away from where people were sleeping, looked promising. I decided to try to get inside one of the smaller tents and circled it slowly looking for a flaw in the taut lines of canvas stretched against the ground. I heard a dog begin to bark by the caravans and froze but the night quiet soon resumed. At the entrance to the tent there was a porch held up by wooden stakes and it was relatively easy to work my fingers underneath and pull it clear of the turf. Inside, my hands met tough rubber mats on the floor and after hauling my body through, I unfolded cautiously onto my feet. All was black. Gingerly I pawed the darkness around me. My eyes widened and strained to make out shapes and definition in the dark but I could make nothing more than a shroud of pale night illumination leaking into the tent. I stood at the mercy of the dark, waiting for my eyes to give me more. Nothing I could understand, just the faintest impression of something ahead. My feet settled on the rubber matting spread across the floor, sending minuscule creaks through it.

"Ali?" An involuntary plea, without any real hope or expectation. My voice, shockingly loud, croaked, alone. The dark gave out no response. Silence.

I remembered the matches in my bag, dropped to my knees and hauled my pack off my back. Inside, my fingers found a forgotten sweater and I pulled it over my head gratefully. Also my toothbrush and a strangely familiar yielding parcel of tin foil. It was the remainder of the cooked sausages I took from mum's fridge before I left! We hadn't finished them that first night by the river after all. How could they have remained forgotten for so long? I placed them carefully to one side; a trace of their stale salty scent perfumed the air: the essence of home.

The matches rattled and the little balsa drawer slid open. I withdrew a match; felt for the non-phosphorus end and struck. Acrid sulphur assaulted my nostrils and a sphere of orange light burst at my fingertips. I gasped. A squat horribly familiar dwarf was grimacing at me. I took half a step back and, in grotesque mimicry, the dwarf did the same. A hall of mirrors! I glanced to my left and a monstrous stretched figure leered at me. Then, a grotesque parade of distortion and horror unfolded around me: dozens of stretched and contorted orange versions of me gyrating in the match light. I allowed myself a grin and held the burning match out towards the nearest little gremlin in front of me. His lumpen head stretched back and his fist dissolved into a lurid lump of flesh. My finger burned and I swore and shook out the match.

The second match took me past a parade of orange distortions: melted twins reaching out to one another, hunched, furtive goblins and gruesome overhanging spectres. I reached the tent's centre, a circle of identical normal mirrors surrounding another small circle of soft chairs, stretched out across two of them and pulled my jacket round myself. It was getting colder and I would need a blanket soon. But I was happy to be undercover and safe. I scoffed the sausages, delicious mementos, and then there was nothing to do but fall asleep again. Tomorrow it would be time to talk to the fair people, see if Ali has been through, but that was tomorrow. Sleep arrived fast, hungry.

Fifteen

THE FOX

Iwoke early, haunted by faces gathering in my dreams: Ali with blood on his hands; Mr Steven Johnston turning slowly away; Macauley showing me the controls of a powerful locomotive and, most disturbingly, the steady gaze of my dad. It was already hot under the canvas and there was a film of sweat between my body and the leather I had been lying on. I gathered up my bag and took a last look at the leering mirrors surrounding me. My hair bulged alarmingly out of the top of my head. I couldn't tell what was distortion and what was real; I guessed I must look a state but a hall of mirrors was the wrong place for an objective view. Anyway, I shrugged, it was nothing to worry about: just another messy boy, nothing more, ready to disappear again. I looked at the imprint of my body on the leather chairs I had slept on. It was already vanishing and soon I would be gone, leaving no trace behind me.

I squeezed under the tent flap, soaking myself in dew in the process, and headed for the river, hoping to pick up the scent of Ali.

On a scrubby patch of grass between the caravans and the river, a group of fairground workers were pulling scaffolding poles off the back of a flatbed. I stood a little off them, waiting, hoping they would notice me, offer some kind words or encouragement. They ignored me. A radio fizzed gently from the cab and I could make out the earnest overtures of

Eddie and the Hotrods. A squat, muscular man with a flat cap pulled down over cruel eyes shouted along enthusiastically. *Do anything you wanna do!*

Well, I will then, I thought. "Excuse me!" The men paused. One of the youths idly balanced a towering pole on his palm. "What d'ya want?" said the eldest mildly. He had a bare chest covered in a wispy coat of white hair.

"I'm looking for a friend. You seen him pass through?"

"Lots of folk passing along the river bank," he said. The group stopped work to marvel at my stupidity.

"Lost ya bum chum have ya?" said the man in the flat cap. His hands were dotted with tattoos. His audience smirked and sniggered.

I shrugged and set off, trying to keep my dignity, their laughter ringing in my ears.

The river path rose to a wide sandy stretch on a raised embankment above the banks and I got up on it, put my head down and walked hard for a few miles, the song still ringing mockingly in my ears. What did I wanna do? Less than a day since Ali had gone and my connection with him, our famous telepathy, I admitted to myself grimly, was well and truly shot. My instinct had told me to follow the river but now the doubts crowded in. Maybe he had gone back to find Brenna, despite everything, I thought, and if he had, well where did that leave me?

The path turned away from the water to allow some smart houses' back gardens to give out directly onto the river. Slowly a village gathered around me and I passed a parade of three or four anonymous shops. A bunch of bananas presented themselves at my elbow, hanging outside a grocers with other fruit and vegetables. Just as I had passed them it occurred to me that they were so close I could have gathered them up easily without breaking my stride. My stomach grumbled encouragingly. But now the moment had passed. I stopped outside a newsagents to look back longingly at the fruit. Hunger rose in my chest like nausea, gripping me, compelling me to act, and on an impulse, I returned to the shop and snatched the fruit. I thought I could hear shouts of outrage as I pelted away from the scene, but I couldn't be sure; the adrenaline was whistling too loudly in my ears.

Taking shelter behind a group of dustbins at the back of some big houses on the edge of the village, I gobbled three bananas on the trot. This is bad, I told myself, as my hunger subsided slightly. It was sloppy, petty thievery, sure to bring the attention of the law down on my head. Not like the artistry of the theft of the meat from Mr. French's mansion. I noticed the sole of my trainer was hanging loose, an exhausted and filthy tongue. I was falling apart. What was I to do now? The scent of Ali had gone cold. Should I follow the river or trek back? I would not go home, I told myself. I would not go home.

I rejoined the path and tried giving myself a great motivational speech, vaguely aping some of the rhetorical features my English teacher had mentioned last year. To move against the river's flow would be a defeat; freedom lies downriver not upstream where the trouble started. We will not be defeated; we will not go home.

But who exactly was we?

No, I admitted, it was just me and the classroom seemed a million miles away.

I followed a wide, sandy track towards the river again, surrounded by trees floating in a forest of lurid bracken. Ahead I made out four figures silhouetted against the dirty blue of the Thames. My stomach lurched. They didn't see me but I knew immediately who they were: the four Didcot boys, miles from home and armed with sticks, hunting. I shrunk into the shelter of the trees at the side of the path. Were they looking for us, looking to avenge Ali's slight in Didcot? Or just foraging for something to do? Four bored kids like Blake, George, Ali and me, looking for their own nook and their own train to assault. They were a long way from home anyway, if Didcot was their home.

I remembered Ali facing them down, I'm your murderer, son. He transformed himself into a hard nut, a man to be feared and deferred to. Maybe, I thought, I could do that too...

Still I decided it was best to avoid them and to give it some time before continuing along the riverbank. I found a clearing where the sea of bracken gave way to a floor of dry bark and hard mud. Sitting with my back to a tree, I listened to the sounds of the woods. Birds chorused inanely, spiralling calls and responses. I closed my eyes and was suddenly transported to the woods near Radley, to Brenna and Squirrel's entrance, the playful aggression of the chucked stone. I missed company.

Somewhere in the bracken I heard an animal stir and my eyes popped open again. A glimpse of red – a fox's tail – a magnificent flourish. Then his nose poked inquisitively out. I sat stock still. The fox had seen me; he was curious but wary, testing the odds, seeing what I would give him. Then he revealed himself, positioning himself side on so I could take in his span. He was long, lean, hungry; his coat impossibly glossy and lush. I smiled: this creature, I thought, thrives on freedom, the call of the wild. His eyes caught mine - deep green pools; they contained wisdom greater than the animal head that held them, greater than me, bigger than all of us.

"Hey boy," I whispered, so soft my lips barely moved.

His ears slid back incrementally. Then he froze again. I noticed a tautness in his haunches. He looked beyond me, towards the river. And then I heard voices, and a shifting and cracking of the bracken. The fox slipped away. Abruptly, the Didcot boy with a blonde crew cut and Chelsea shirt burst into the clearing, holding a shred of toilet paper in his left hand. It was the runt from Sip Smoker's gang, their George, come to shit in my clearing. He didn't see me, resting motionless against the tree, and got immediately to his urgent business, ripping his trousers down, obviously desperate for relief. I could have sprang up and let him have it; a quick succession of punches to his fat, stupid face. He was weaker than me and would have been unable, with his trousers round his ankles, to put up any sort of fight. But, I realised, he still would have shouted out, even if I had been able to deal with him quickly, and that would bring Sip Smoker and the other two to his aid. So I stayed where I was, sinking my back into the bark, willing myself invisible. The boy screwed up his face and squeezed. A foul whiff ghosted my nostrils. Finishing, he remained hunched for a moment, letting the muscles in his face relax and his eyes go blank. Then, as he gathered his senses again, his eyes wandered around the clearing and came to rest...on me. His eyes widened and stayed wide; his mouth closed, jaw tightened. I stayed stock still. Maybe, I thought, he would think me dead, or some sort of hallucination. Maybe he would rejoin his friends, keep our encounter to himself, too complex and bizarre a scenario to deal with. I could see the cogs in his mind turning; he had a choice: either holler for his friends with his trousers still down or clean himself in front of me. I stayed exactly where I was, keeping the impetus with him.

"What are you doing?" he muttered finally. He was confused and, I could see now, unnerved. I had him cornered, exposed. I continued to stare neutrally into the distance. Suddenly he stood up, pulling his trousers up around him, leaving his arse dirty. With a last hard glare in my direction, half hostility, half confusion, he bolted into the bracken.

I needed to move. I took off fast in the opposite direction, running through the woods away from the river. I couldn't see where I was placing my feet because of the waist high sea of green and a couple of times my foot fell into empty space instead of meeting the ground as I hit a pothole. I turned an ankle, felt it jar, but I couldn't stop, I had to get away from my pursuers. I stole a glance behind. Sip Smoker was thrashing through the bracken after me in a black tracksuit top. Adrenaline, sheer fright, burned in my lungs and sang in my ears. And then I was falling. Hard onto the ground. The bracken crashed and splintered around my ears. My ankle seized. My flight was over.

They were all standing over me within minutes. Sip Smoker first on the scene. He treated me to a cruel grin and lit up a cigarette. He was not particularly out of breath, his chest rising and falling just slightly more than it might usually, a slight reediness in the exhalation of his smoke. His three charges arrived together a minute or so after, noisily panting and grunting with approval at the sight of their quarry rendered helpless.

"Where's ya mate now then?" said Tall Boy. "Didn't think you'd be running into us again, did ya?"

"He'll be sorry he did," added the boy with the freckled face. "Coytey," he asked the lad in the Chelsea shirt, "did ya finish ya crap?"

"Crapped," said Coytey bashfully, "ain't finished though." He held up the unused toilet paper apologetically. Tall boy and freckle face chuckled in gleeful disgust.

"Wipe ya arse then wipe it on him," said Freckle Face tentatively, as if he was not sure if his suggestion might be seen as too disgusting by the others. Sip shrugged, as if such an act might be below him, but the others goaded on Chelsea shirt who disappeared into the bracken to finish his business.

"I asked you where your mate is," demanded Tall Boy again, "him with the big mouth." He landed a half kick half stamp on my upper arm that felt immediately impossibly painful, as if my bones were splintering and ripping into my flesh. Tears crowded my eyes, rendering the world bleary, soft focus.

"Please, I don't know where he is," I pleaded. Another kick, this time in my chest. I didn't know who it was from but it hurt even worse than the last. I spluttered and gasped for breath. My mouth was full of blood, or vomit or thick spittle,

I didn't know which. And then the kicks came in fast and hard and all I could hear was Sip Smoker's direction, calmly calling the name of my next assailant and his instructions on where to hurt me: Dean, back, good, now leg, dead leg; Matt; ribs, yes; Dean, don't kick him in the head, might kill him or knock him brain dead, punch him, like that, yes that's it, again; Coytey! Your turn son, ribs, stomach...

I drifted off, somehow the pain faded; my body became a shell and I got lost inside it. Their blows echoed on my exterior and I imagined myself lying in an empty rusty water tank the outside of which someone was beating furiously but harmlessly with a stick.

Finally, I wondered aimlessly, almost with amusement, whether they would actually smear Coytey's shit on my face.

Sixteen

GONE TO GROUND

I lay on my back in my tank for a long time. There was a faint smell of dead water and a rusty taste of dried blood on my palate but mainly there was just nothing, just darkness and the ever-so-faint whisper of my breath. I was lying in a half inch of soothing rainwater; the wetness soaked into my clothes and nursed my wounds gently. I lay dead still. It is very important, I told myself, that I did not move, not even an inch, not even a millimetre. Just one over-heavy breath was enough to remind me of the injuries to my left upper arm and in my chest. Any real movement led to a searing, ripping pain, splintered bone tearing into tender flesh. Something was broken, something fundamentally wrong. It was best just to lie there and wait until the pain subsided.

Then I heard the rhythm of another breath. It ran parallel to mine, but deeper, ruder, harsher. And through the dank air a heavy smell broke through, wet fur, warm carnivorous body. The fox. I was not in a tank. I was lying in the bracken still, abandoned by Sip Smoker's gang, left for dead. My eyes were shut tight. It was not dark at all. Well, I didn't know, it might have been. I couldn't get my lids to open. The fox was very close to my face. His breath smelt unmistakably of meat; I recognised the flat taste of fat and bone from butchers' shops. He had just eaten. Then his breath quickened, and a whisker brushed my cheek. Somewhere inside me, an alarm sounded.

I realised this creature might feed on my face unless I stopped him. My eyelids cracked painfully when I forced them open, they were welded together with dried blood, pus and tears. I saw the deep green pools of the fox's eyes up close and saw they were inquisitive not hungry. Slowly, his bushy red flush of tail rose behind him, giving him a fuller presence.

"Hey, boy," I murmured. He was not afraid. He regarded me steadily, patiently, waiting for my next move. I raised my right arm; it was not as painful as my left. "Hurt bad, boy," I told the fox. A drop of rain fell on my face. Then one landed right on the end of the soft black leather of the fox's nose. I propped myself onto my right elbow and shifted my body. My chest hurt bad, bruised or broken ribs maybe. I let loose a moan and the fox was gone. A sudden sprawl of rain sprayed my face as I lurched to a sit up position, cradling my injured left arm in my right, broken for sure, at the top, under my shoulder. The slightest movement sent a lightning bolt of raw pain shooting through me, filling my stomach full of sickness and jarring at my teeth. A rain sprawl again. If I stayed where I was, I would be soaked through. Got to go. Somewhere. Anywhere.

On my feet, the pain was containable. I made my right arm into a cushioned sling for my left, ready to absorb any jolts from below and set off through the woods in the direction I was running when Sip had caught up with me, away from the river. My progress was slow; I picked my way through the bracken cagily, trying to avoid disturbing my ribs and upper arm. Of course it was impossible and several times I stopped to whimper in pain and frustration. Somewhere within me anger rose, and I used it for fuel to feed my uncertain progress. I needed to find someone to blame for this pain. The rain slid down my face now and I used my good arm to wipe it dry. Easy maybe to hate Chelsea shirt and the raw stupidity of the tall kid. Somehow impossible to hate Sip Smoker. It would be like hating the fox because, like the fox, he was only following his nature.

Gibberish was spinning round my head as I picked my way to the edge of the woods. The anger I was feeling went Ali's way. He wound up Sip Smoker, he let George take him and he killed Blake. And then he left me. It wasn't fair me blaming him, I knew that. He had saved us from a beating at the gate at Didcot, he couldn't help George getting the better of him and he didn't mean to drop Blake unconscious in the lock. But still, but still...

I lurched across a field. Several cows eyed me wearily, monochrome hides gleaming in the rain. Piss off, I hissed at them. Piss off cows! Piss off! They stared back balefully, great mournful brown eyes absorbing my ire. Sorry, I whispered, sorry cows.

There was a line of big houses at the other side of the field and I staggered towards them. Their rear windows gave out onto the field and I imagined the people who lived there would see me hobbling through the cow field like some stumbling casualty of war. I didn't care anymore; I was willing to give myself up to the houses and the road I decided, whatever it would bring. The rain had been steadily increasing and I was soaked through. My teeth chattered and rattled my arm, and I cried out in pain and frustration. Finally, the word I had never said slid out easily, willingly. Help. Just a whisper at first. Then a cracked, choking plea. "Help," I called to the rain, to the sullen backs of houses, to the dirty road, "help me."

The field ended in a fence with a neat doorway leading into the back garden of one of the houses. The handle turned loosely in my hand. Locked. Where to now? I was ready to give up: broken, beaten and soaked to the skin, there was nothing left of me. I slumped against the door and the pain racked through my upper body. I mumbled all the swear words I knew to myself softly, trying to stitch a lullaby out of the wet and the hurt, passed out for a time, then woke shivering and lost. I scrambled to my feet, not sure how much time had passed and then I saw a rusty piece of steel lying by the fence and without hesitation, impatiently, used it to jimmy my way into the door, forcing the lock. The wood splintered and cracked and then I was standing in a garden, neat and tidy in the fresh, glistening rainfall.

The lights in the house were off. I dry retched, staggering and lurching on the lawn like a drunk, but no sick came. Then I came to my senses a little and closed the broken door behind me. There was a garage tacked onto the house with a door leading onto the garden and this time this door opened without being forced.

A boat, strapped to a trailer with its top tightly sealed by a tarp, took up the almost all the space inside. I shook horribly, teeth chattering. I wanted to be discovered, arrested, rehabilitated but there was nothing here except the rattle of more rainfall on the roof. The boat reminded me of my fugitive's dream, sleeping on Spanish beaches with Ali, dusting the sand off our bodies and blinking in the heat of the morning as we woke to another day of freedom, to an escape made good.

I shook off the vision and looked around me. The garage was well equipped. There were several ladders lying across the rafters in the roof and the walls were lined with tools, clothing and shelves heaving with tins and bottles. A white racing bicycle hung at one end of a long wall and a set of golf clubs hung at the other. I stood quivering for a minute or so and then put on a heavy sou'wester I found on a hook on the wall and peeled off the sopping wet things I had on underneath. Then I unhooked the tarp along the boat's side and pulled up a chair so I could ever so carefully lean into the boat to take a look. It smelt of oil and rope, a solid satisfying aroma. I threw my wet clothes inside and grabbed a solid looking rubber cased torch I found hanging on the wall with the tools. Then I slowly tipped myself into the boat trying hard not to jar my sore arm and ribs. I managed to lower myself onto the floor without sending too much pain shooting through my upper body and arm and hung my clothes over the polished planks put in for seating. Then I pulled the tarp back over the boat's side, folded myself onto its floor and waited for my shivering to stop. Slowly the frenzied chattering subsided, giving way to occasional deep, prolonged shivers which then stopped altogether.

Then I rolled against something hard which dug into my back and I turned to see a little doorway, a hatch into the stern. Inside was a nest of cushions and blankets. I secreted myself in this dark hideaway, an animal gone to ground, and felt unconsciousness fold around me.

Seventeen

THE WORM

Swimming through the filth of the canal, I scan the lock basin for Blake. The light, leaking through the surface, cuts, breaks and refracts in the gloom, sending broken rods of sickly yellow beams through the water, spotlighting floating debris, sweet wrappers, rat shit, condoms. My hands come together as in prayer and I push them into the murk, then pull them back, propelling my torso forward. I have no need of lungs. Oxygen is reaching my blood by other means. Maybe I have gills, ghastly slots in my neck drawing some life out of this mire, but it really doesn't matter. Nothing matters apart from finding Blake. I look for signs of his hideous corpse rolling in the deep, a strewn limb, a dead eye, a lock of blonde hair.

Yes. A lock of honey blonde hair. Here he is. The hair twists in the weeds, gently waving as my swimming stirs up the dead water around his body. He lies face down in his watery bed, boots still intact.

I hover above him and his body tilts in the gloom. He turns around to face me. His eyes are closed; his face peaceful in sleep, in death. All his tyranny and his cruelty have melted away on the softness of his skin. A water baby. An innocent boy. And we killed him. A shard of guilt pierces my guts.

"Blake," I whisper, "Blake, are you there?"

His eyes open. Horrified, I'm staring into the steely blue

149

of our leader's eyes. All my compassion disappears, the fear returns and Blake sees it in me. He grins hideously. "Rich," he says, "you killed me."

"We didn't mean to kill you," I say. "It was self-defence."

"Bull," says Blake. "Murder is what you did."

George, sitting passively in the gloom behind his brother, nods in solemn satisfaction. "Know what they do to murders? 'Specially child killers?" continues Blake, enjoying my discomfort, "lock 'em up for life, square little cell, metal toilet, hard bunk, one blanket. That's what you'll get. I'd rather be dead."

"But you're not even dead," I shout as Blake and George begin to laugh, "are you? Are you?"

"I dunno," says Blake, "ask him."

He points towards the surface and I see a worm, writhing on a gleaming hook. The worm? He wants me to ask the worm? Then I follow the line upwards, beyond the surface and see Macaulay surrounded by fishing equipment, staring impassively at his line.

Eighteen

THE MORTIMERS

When I woke I was cold, sore and desperate for a piss. Visions of Blake's talking corpse hung over me like a sickness. I lay awake listening to the sound of rain on the roof of the garage for a while, safe in my cushioned cupboard, and then, satisfied that no one was about, clambered out of the boat. I examined the white racing bicycle hanging on the wall, letting my hands glide over the smooth, skinny tires and the furry tape on the drop bars. Then the need to piss got so urgent I was jigging about on my haunches and sending shooting pains up my arm. I let myself out of the garage.

A drizzly dawn had shrouded the garden in a flat, grey half light. All the houses in this row had their lights off, a ghost street; a few crows cawed aimlessly and a car buzzed emptily away on the main road. I took a quiet piss in the bushes at the side of the garden, looking through the glass of patio doors into the living room of the house as I did. It looked comfortable, if a bit stuffy, a generous powder blue sofa, a mantel adorned with family photographs. My upper arm throbbed urgently and my ribs ached steadily as my breath drew in and out.

Inside, I got to work on the door leading from the kitchen into the house. I found a lump hammer and used it to smack one end of a chisel until its other end was wedged in between the frame and the door. I made plenty of noise as I worked.

I didn't care if the neighbours heard me; in fact it would have come as a relief at this stage. I wasn't about to give myself up but I didn't have a plan for staying on the run either. There was no way forward now, so I threw myself into the hands of fate. Eventually, with a sickening splintering of wood, the frame came away from the door. All this effort had made my injuries howl insistently and, as I stood contemplating the wreckage of the door, I wondered if inside me broken ribs were slowly skewering vital organs.

Anyway despite making a right mess and messing up my insides, the door remained intact; it was time to raise the stakes. There were some power tools hanging on the wall at the back of the garage, flexes neatly coiled behind them. A small chainsaw looked too brutal, a heavy drill too cumbersome. But a handheld jigsaw seemed promising. I found a tray of neatly ordered drill bits and blades in a draw beneath the weapon and fitted the heaviest, roughest looking blade. Then, making a gruesome racket, I ground a rough rectangle out of the bottom of the door, making an opening big enough for me to crawl through. Now, I reflected with satisfaction, I would have definitely raised the alarm and I paused, contemplating the view of kitchen floor tiles showered with sawdust I had created, waiting for the shouts or the knocks or the sirens that surely must come.

Nothing. The parched silence of this forgotten corner of Berkshire continued, broken only by the occasional murmur of a distant car engine. I crawled carefully through my hatch and stood up in a large, square kitchen with a wooden table and cream, uncluttered work surfaces. A window looked out onto the awakening garden and a digital clock blinked on a fitted cooker. 05:36. I felt an animal shrill of satisfaction. Shelter. Food. There was not much in the fridge, a small cube of hardening cheddar and a half full bottle of dubious looking milk, so I guessed the homeowners were away. I peeled back the foil cap at the top of the bottle. It smelt neutral but looked too thick to be drinkable. I put it back then carried out a rapid inventory of supplies, swinging open cupboard doors, checking shelves and rooting through drawers. Nothing much fresh but possibilities for meals certainly. There were some tins of soup, tomatoes and beans, rice and pasta in glass jars, half a dozen onions that looked fine and a bag of potatoes sprouting grotesque opaque shoots.

Time to check the rest of the house. There was the lounge I saw from outside, anonymously comfortable, a dining room and three bedrooms upstairs. It was a tidy house, clean and functional, the boat the only real indulgence. Photographs around the house told a story: a man held his mortar board onto a thatch of dark curls as a gust of unruly wind in a seaside town attempted to remove it; later the same man was older, hair shorter, and smiling shyly beside a slight bird like young woman. I felt a stab of guilt. What was I doing in these people's house?

Just surviving, I told myself, shrugging off the guilt.

Downstairs by the kitchen was a yachting calendar pinned to the wall with the month of August open and a picture of a flashy looking craft, anchored up in a serene Mediterranean inlet. The dates for the last week of August were crossed through in blue biro with the word 'Cahors' neatly printed in the same blue ink above the line. Whose hand? As I suspected the occupants of this house were away on holiday. I turned to September; they were due back on the 1st. But when was now? I turned on the radio just in time to hear six long beeps and the date. Wednesday the 24th of August. If I wanted to, I realised, I could hole up here for over a week. Relief washed over me and then, with hands shaking in anticipation, I put a kettle on, chopped an onion, pushed sticks of spaghetti into the boiling water, added a tin of tomatoes to the frying onion and then, when it was soft, tipped in the spaghetti too. Finally I crumbled in the lump of cheese. I ate my feast standing up, straight out of the pan. I was so hungry, so spent, that every mouthful tasted like heaven. It is still the best meal I've ever had but with the last mouthful came a wash of memory: home, mum's spaghetti sauce.

I found out that the house belonged to Frank and Beryl Mortimer. They were on holiday in a house near Cahors in southern France with their grown-up son, Richard, the man in the photographs upstairs, and his pregnant wife, Caroline. Hungry for evidence of normality, of other people's lives, I looked through some of their things, sketching out their lives from the fragments of the house, adding detail with each letter, picture or document. Frank's pristine and pressed uniform in a cupboard in one of the spare bedrooms led me on a trail to investigate his time in the navy. He served in the Second World War in the Far East and the South Pacific: Hong Kong, Jakarta, Bombay. I found letters from Frank to his new wife in a shoe box in a cupboard in the same room. I read about Frank's meals aboard the HMS Pepperpot, the 'indeterminate meat and cabbage', the surprising ingredients to be found in the soup and the anticipation and mild satisfaction caused by Saturday's jam sponge puddings. There was also considerable coverage of his roommate's battles with a bladder infection and his fortunes in the games of cribbage the officers played on Saturday nights. The ports his ship visited were always described with disgust, their streets, 'teeming with beggars' and 'hapless devils', the food inedible and everything always enveloped in claustrophobic heat.

Bored of Frank's travels, I turned on the TV but there was nothing on. Just the test card: the smug girl playing noughts and crosses with her grotesque clown doll. Some fiddly jazz tinkled away and I stared moronically at the image for a while. Then I hauled some cushions onto the floor and made a bed to rest my ribs and arm.

I let my eyes close momentarily but Blake was there straight away. Instead I stared at the books on the Mortimers' shelves. Victor Hugo, Lamb's Tales from Shakespeare, Frederick Forsyth. What am I doing here? I thought. I needed to get mended and back on the road. An hour passed. Still the test card and the never ending jazz. I was in some sort of daze, losing my mind. Eventually I picked myself up and walked vacantly around the house, then went out to the garage and looked for a while at the bicycle again. It had a tiny hard saddle and blue furry tape round the drop bars. A means of escape? But where to ride to? The trail to Ali had gone cold. I didn't know if he was following the river anymore, didn't know anything instinctively anymore; my sixth sense, my conviction that I was thinking and feeling the same as my friend had gone, kicked out of me by Sip Smoker's gang and Ali's betrayal. I knew, though, that once my direction was set, this bicycle would be my means of travel. It was faster, would be smoother on my battered ribs, allowing me more opportunities to find my friend.

I looked down at my hands, at the dirt under my nails and the filth caked up the wrists. I was filthy. I probably stank too but somehow you don't smell yourself even when your stench is repulsing others. I went upstairs to the bathroom, the white and blue décor in keeping with the prim order elsewhere, and nearly shouted out in shock. In the mirror, a dirty, surly youth clapped his hand to his mouth as I felt my own hand smack against my lips. My eye and lips were eruptions of purple, my hair unkempt, grown out and tangled. My face streaked with dirt and there was something, a thin wisp of willowy fluff under my nose and shadowing my cheeks that looked a bit like beard. I leant into the glass for a closer inspection and the leering thug bent towards me. My face seemed obscured, as if covered in cobwebs. But under the dirt was a map of my journey. Grimy dirt from sleeping rough shaded my brow and neck and a few rouge freckles peppered my cheeks. I had never had freckles; I stared at them in astonishment. Then I examined the damage Sip Smoker's gang had visited on my face. My eye was raised, purple and reptilian, as if a purple frog was trying to climb out of the socket, and my lip thick, split and blue. I was a hideous picture: the Mortimers would have been horrified to find me in their house. The damage was complimented by two giant spots, one on my forehead and one on my nose. The pressure on the skin holding these red welts in check was palpable. And yes, there were the beginnings of a cobweb beard and moustache, a ghostly shadow. I looked again at the Quasimodo leering at me and in the end took some heart from my loathsome appearance. I felt the tough kid on the run, Ali's mate, returning and flashed the mirror a faked rugged smile.

I plugged the bath, slung both taps on full and undressed. My damaged upper arm was a mess of yellow and purple, but my ribs looked encouragingly normal. I found a bottle of blue bubble bath and threw it in; bubbles climbed above the surface.

I got into the bath, letting the delicious hot water encase my body and ducked my head beneath the water.

Soapy silence.

The lock.

I fought the urge to resurface, to escape the trauma of the drowning. Instead, I forced my eyes open. They stung in the soapy water but I stubbornly kept them open, picking out the murky shape of my body, the pink of my arm, the haze of the porcelain bath.

Carefully I raised my right hand, balled it into a fist and slammed it back into the water. Blake's body, felled by Ali's knockout punch. I could see it. Sinking. I watched my fist drift helpless to the bottom of the tub.

Now my left fist, me. A crash as it broke the surface. And again, Ali. The fist moved purposefully, looking for Blake. It could not see him. It headed upwards again, starved of air.

I surfaced, George staring at me, his face swollen, grotesque, like a cheap rubber toy.

"He can't swim!"

Ali beside me, panic in his eyes.

"You see him?"

He shook his head and dived again, deep this time. His feet emerged, then propelled him deep into the water. I followed.

But now the right fist, up until now drifting helplessly in the murk, was recovering, moving on the opposite side of the bath towards its edge, towards an iron ladder leading to the concrete path on the opposite side of the lock from where his brother stood. The two swimmers searched the lock floor for him, but Blake has found his swimmer's legs, his impetus to survive. He grasps the side of the ladder and hauls himself up it, driven by the need to breathe again, to live.

My right hard emerged from the bathwater.

Alive.

It climbed out of the water through the bubbles and secreted itself, ashamed, behind a collection of shampoo bottles.

And George saw a ghost emerge from the murky canal. Blake, dizzy, clambered up the last ladder steps onto the concrete edge of the lock; he rolled away from the lock, panting and choking. But alive. Alive.

"Blake!" hollered George. He had seen his brother defeated, nearly killed. Now he didn't know what to do.

"Go! Run!" screamed the ghost, horrified at his humiliation. And George obeyed, he ran.

My left fist had been under the bathwater for around thirty seconds. Two ripples as it came up. Ali and I broke the surface. But when we looked at the path, George was gone. We both swam to the side. He was running away back up the tow path, back towards his house.

"George!" I screamed, "George!"

He stopped. He turned and looked beyond us to check we didn't have Blake then he was off again, running away from the scene.

We hauled ourselves out of the water. We were both quivering, neither of us knew whether it was through cold or through fear but we convulsed as we stood pathetically on the spot, teeth chattering, dripping relentlessly on the grass. We both looked back at the lock but all is still.

But Blake had rolled out of sight in the long grass bordering the lock. Beaten and humiliated.

And the two boys, Richard and Ali, turned and ran away too.

I smiled. A story. Probably not true.

But it could have happened like that.

Feeling inexplicably cheered, I dried myself off with a fresh towel from the airing cupboard and returned downstairs wearing a navy toweling robe. My arm and ribs felt easier after my soak and my head felt lightened, unburdened by the possibility of Blake escaping death. It was only an idea though, I told myself sternly, and a far-fetched one at that.

I watched TV mindlessly for a few hours, using the words and pictures as a numbing balm, a tapestry of comforting nonsense. I noticed a barely discernible ticking coming from my bag, still lying unpacked beside me on the floor. My watch, stopped since Blake was lost in the lock, had come back to life. Another sign! I watched the incremental progress of the second hand in wonder, a smile creeping across my chops. More nonsense of course but I clambered upstairs to the Mortimers' spare bedroom strangely pacified. I folded my weary, damaged and bruised body into the crisp cotton of the clean sheets and collapsed into a colossal dreamless sleep.

Nineteen

COINTREAU

I slept through till the next afternoon, woke rested and, although my wounds ached hard, I felt much less damaged, more whole. I wriggled the fingers of my left hand in front of my face. Maybe my arm was not broken after all.

Ravenous again, I made my way downstairs in the striped dressing gown to see what I could find to eat. I pulled the sprouts off the potatoes, sliced them and fried them up. The Mortimers had olive oil too, just like mum, so I used plenty of that. I looked thoughtfully at the green telephone on a small table in the hall with a low padded seat next to it. I knew two numbers by heart, my home number and Macaulay's. I could reach out at any time and connect either with the lopsided familiarity of my home life or with the dangerous world of Macaulay. I considered home first. Being in the house, wrapped in the fusty comfort of the Mortimers, had served a purpose but I felt guilt for the distress my damage would bring these people when they returned from holiday and it reminded me too of the comforts of *my* home. What I wouldn't do, I thought, to sit in my own lounge and watch the TV, maybe help mum make a delicious supper. But I couldn't yet. There was too much that needed solving first. And that brought me to Macaulay. Could he help me find Ali and would he let me know what had happened with Blake? He had said he would help me. And he had shown us he could find people, he had found us after all, walking at night miles from home. Maybe he would be able to track Ali down too. He claimed to work instinctively, a lone operator, not an ordinary policeman, a special agent, as he'd said. How could I use him and keep myself safe? If I called him, I thought, maybe I could maybe gauge the possibilities.

Too much to think about. I wallowed in front of the box watching the children's programmes, growing older with every hour, Playschool, Jackanory, Blue Peter. When the news started up I watched that too but there was nothing about me or Ali or Blake. Space probes, riots in Birmingham, a machine printing pound notes but nothing about missing boys or drowned boys or any boys. I felt disappointment and a little indignation. Why didn't anyone care? Why weren't they looking for us? One measly police boat, a botched raid on a traveler site, the twisted Macaulay. Surely the world cared more than that. The last item on the news four days ago and we were off the agenda. Surely we were worth more than that.

Chief inspector James Fletcher admitted the boys could be anywhere in the country now and may even have escaped abroad. He refused to rule out the possibility of abduction but said the boys were more likely to have run away.

How could that be good enough? I thought, dismissed by a bunch of bumbling fools. And Blake was dead so the coppers were letting a couple of murderers slip away. If he was dead... my dreams and far out theories weren't enough to disregard the evidence of still water and a missing boy. Somehow getting away with it was more terrifying than not.

Like Brenna said: *Odds are against you but don't mean you won't win out. If you get away, proper away, lose yourself a long way from here, you can get away with it. You wouldn't be the first.*

Suddenly, I missed Ali keenly, strongly, an acid burn of longing, like a slug of whiskey from Wild Bill's bottle.

And in response I was at the teak drinks bureau in the Mortimers' lounge examining the array of bottles, looking for the antidote to the pain, just like Wild Bill had all his life. I picked up a bottle of whiskey, a Scottish single malt, and took a big slug straight from the neck. A grenade exploded in my mouth. It tasted as if made of petrol and carpet cleaner but it contained a sweet punch; and somewhere deep in the mix of this acid soup, was the rich scent of cornfields. Once my mouth had recovered, I think I felt some numbing, some lessening of the hurt. Encouraged, I tried some other bottles, standing like a greedy partygoer helping himself to the buffet. I didn't worry about the open curtains; I was back in kamikaze mode. Come and catch me, I thought, as I swigged poison from the cool necks, I don't care. Gin: fairly disgusting but more palatable than the whiskey. Vodka: not too bad but hardly pleasant. Cointreau: actually quite nice, a deep orange burn. I took several deep slugs of that one.

The bottle was two thirds full when I picked it up and by the time I placed it carefully on the floor, it was two thirds empty. I felt light headed and silly. I hiccupped and let a deep cavernous belch loose.

Then I called home.

I listened to the ringing emptily droning in my ear, forgetting myself and what I was doing.

"Hello?" said Beth.

They were watching The Liver Birds. And so was I. Well at least it was on my TV; I had the sound down. I could hear the sound chiming along with my pictures in perfect unison.

"Hello?" said Beth again. Then, warily, tentatively, "Rich?"

I could hear mum too. She said, who is it?

"Rich, is that you?" said Beth, "are you there?"

I was just enjoying hearing their voices; a lazy grin spread over my face.

"Rich!" shouted Beth, "Rich, if that's you; you have to let us know you're all right. We've been worried sick..."

"I'm OK. I'm really fine. Just let mum know I've got some business to sort out..."

"Business?" Incredulous Beth was back in my life. I smiled dreamily to myself. Beth had chanced upon a boy of such stupidity she could hardly believe it. "Where on earth are you Rich? Are you drunk?"

"I'm not drunk," I said but realised I was slurring my words as I said them. "I am not drunk," I said as slowly as I could.

"What the hell are you doing, Rich? Hang on, I'm putting mum on."

"No."

"Richard," said mum. Her voice was faint, the imprint of a breath. I couldn't bear it. Tears welled up inside me and I opened my mouth but only a parched croak emerged. I should have asked Beth about Blake, but it was too late and I certainly couldn't ask mum. My throat clicked again, an empty magazine. And now frustration surged up through the pain and the guilt. I hated myself, the whole pathetic mess. I hurtled the receiver down into its cradle and then, too late, I finally found my voice. A roaring groan of unhappiness gushed up from within me. Still no words; only pain, only pain.

I reached for the medicine, the Cointreau, and lost myself in a sickly blur of orange sedation. Delirious, I rolled around the Mortimer's carpet, cursing at the phone and ranting at the photographs.

Then, finally, I think - I am not sure about this bit - I reached for the phone again.

And dialed the Oxford code.

Zero.

Eight.

Six.

Five.

Then a five, a one, my house turned around.

A zero in the middle.

Then Ali's turned backwards too: a four and a two.

Somewhere in the Oxford area, in the middle of a late

August evening, a phone began to ring.

Twenty

THE ASHTRAY

Macaulay had been waiting. He was sitting patiently in front of the square table with the overhead light, his elbows planted on the table, his palms open. He wore a black long sleeved round-necked shirt that made him look younger and thinner and lent him the serious, reflective air of a priest. I sat down opposite him, clumsily pulling and spinning the chair out and squeezing myself in front of him. He studied me carefully, calmly, absolutely composed.

"Why did you call?" he asked. He picked up his packet of number 10s from the table, not offering me one this time, and rested a cigarette against his bottom lip, holding it loosely in place with his top one. He sparked it up using a disposable lighter with a worn image of a woman in a swimsuit on it and let the smoke drift in between his lips as he waited for my answer.

"You said you could help," I said helplessly. My gaze bounced off his impenetrable features. "Is Blake dead?"

Macaulay grinned wryly to himself. "I thought you'd worked that one out for yourself," he said.

"I don't know." The cigarette smoke was making me gag and the light seemed draining, inexplicably hot. "I don't know anything. I imagined...dreamt he climbed out of the lock, when we were in it, looking for him."

I looked up into Macaulay's eyes. He was strong, a man's

man; he looked at me with a ghost of faint amusement dancing behind his eyes. "You don't know what's real anymore, do you Richard?"

"No," I said, indignant, "that's why I'm asking you."

"Even if Blake escaped," said Macaulay, "you still can't go home."

"Ali..."

"Ali, yes," he said, "still thinks he is a guilty man, perhaps he is."

"Where is he?"

"Where do you think he is, Richard?"

"You're useless," I shouted, suddenly frustrated by his evasiveness, "what's the point if you won't tell me anything?"

"Not useless. Not useless at all." Macaulay stubbed his fag out in a small round ashtray and looked at me complacently, enjoying my discomfort. "You know that Richard."

"What the hell does that mean?" I can feel my rage rising now. "I'm not in charge of this. Just tell me whether he's dead or not. And tell me where Ali is?"

"Where do you think he is?"

Suddenly I was on my feet and had my hands round Macaulay's throat. His strong hands came up to grab my wrists, to loosen the pressure on his neck, to prise my thumbs out of his windpipe. But I was too strong, there was too much rage, blowing like a gale inside me. Macaulay shrunk, diminished and I let go of his neck and watched in horror as his body folded to the floor.

I woke in the Mortimers' spare bedroom sweating and spooked. The first thing I noticed was the sickness: my head throbbed, my mouth was sawdust dry and my guts pitched and heaved. This then was a hangover. I wondered how the hell people put up with them. But there was worse: these grotesque nightmares and daydreams, these haunting visions of Blake and Macaulay, so vivid, so real, were driving me crazy.

What is real? What is true? I was losing my mind, I told my-self as calmly as I could; I needed help.

The phone began to ring, steadily, insistently.

A stinging recollection: I called home last night. I spoke to Beth and mum. Mum spoke to me. Oh Christ, what did I say?

I got up to look at the phone. It was sitting where I left on the living room floor. Ring ring. Ring ring. It wouldn't stop.

And as I stared at it a further terrible truth emerged, a burning revelation. I had called Macaulay too the previous night. I stood with my hand cupped over my mouth. What the hell had I told him?

Still it rang.

I lifted the receiver and pressed the little button under-neath. Finally the ringing ceased. Thank God.

Then vomit rose suddenly and violently from my stom-ach and I ran, hand over my mouth to the kitchen sink and spewed a foul, noxious black liquid with the look and consis-tency of old engine oil all over the Mortimers' stainless steel sink unit. Then I leant panting and spent with my hands on the edge of the sink and my ribs smarting in pain. Dizzy, sud-denly tired and defeated, I limped back upstairs to the Mor-timers' spare room.

As I drifted off into some sort of sleep again, the phone began again. I pulled two pillows over my head. Somehow I managed to block everything out.

A few hours later, I was awake again. The phone was still ringing. In a daze, I staggered out of bed and stared at it. Eventually, this time of its own accord, it stopped.

I spent an hour in the bathroom nursing my wounds. I showered and found a bottle of witch hazel to dab my bruises with. They seemed to be healing anyway. The bruising in the ribs had come through now, a deep flush of purple and blue; and my arm was almost certainly not broken after all, just hid-eously bruised. I didn't feel ready to go just yet though. The more I thought about it the more I knew that it was Macaulay calling. And he could only be calling me if he didn't know where I was. But maybe, I thought, if I didn't answer he won't know where I am. Had I told him where I was? Maybe blurted out some telling information. I didn't know. Most likely thing is, I decided, he can return my calls but doesn't know where I am.

Seeking strength, I breakfasted on a tin of beans heated on the hob, wishing I had some bread and some bacon to go with them. Immediately my head and guts felt better. If I was going to run, where would I run to? Did I know where Ali was? I tried to think logically. I had been right before; he wouldn't have wanted to retrace his steps.

Unless it was to find Brenna.

The obvious truth that I hadn't wanted to face before stared back at me. Of course Ali was with Brenna. But not back towards Oxford. I tried to recall what Brenna had said as we walked away from the second site towards Wallingford. She had mentioned going abroad, Ireland, France, Spain. And Windsor too. Windsor. There was a map on the Mortimers' shelves and I spread it out on the kitchen table. Soon I could work out where I was, a village called Thornton, 14 miles away from Windsor, possible on the white racer certainly.

The bike was still hanging on the wall of the garage. It looked uncomfortable but impressive, streamlined with drop bars, a hard raised saddle and bright adornments of tape and stickers. I tried lifting it with my right arm. It was feather light and I could easily lift it off the wall and onto the floor. I tried it gingerly for size, leaning the bars against the wall and hoisting myself onto the pedals in the narrow space between the boat and the wall. The saddle was too high. I dismounted and rolled up the garage door to give myself a little more room to work on it. A tall hedge bordered the driveway but I could see a few cars drift by as I stood there, blinking in the sunlight. I found a ring spanner that fitted the nut under the saddle stem and lowered the seat so it was level with my hip.

Back in the house the phone began to go again, this time I marched in and picked up the receiver with a business-like air. But I didn't say anything.

Whoever was on the other end was silent too for some time. We played a game of chicken. Who would speak first? Him. "Frank Mortimer?" Macaulay: a nightmare come true. Blood screamed in my ears.

Finally I composed myself enough to produce a ridiculous accent, comedy posh, ludicrous. "He's not here. He's on holiday."

"Richard?" He sounded curt, impatient, a busy man. I was immediately taken back to the rec, to my timid surrender. But this time he couldn't reach me. He knew my number but he didn't know where I was. And I was bigger and braver than the feckless boy he had caught that night on the meadow.

"Did we speak last night?"

"Of course we did you little fool. Were you so drunk you can't remember? I'm coming to help you, as we arranged." The pathetic, pleading figure begging Ali and me to let him help us had gone. But so too was the authoritative disciplinarian from the rec and the equivocating interviewer from my dream. Macaulay it seemed was a man of many guises; this one was a curt, impatient figure, a man with far better things to do than help a hapless runaway.

"Do you know where I am?"

"No. I need…"

I smiled, glad to have that advantage still and cut him off. "You said you would be able…might help us."

A minor hesitation, maybe a couple of seconds. "We help our friends, Richard, certainly. But we have to be sure they are really our friends." He paused again, allowing me to adjust to the idea of negotiation. "I think it really would be best if we met face to face, Richard, I find it very difficult to talk on the phone." And I could see that. Macaulay, I realised, derived most of his authority from his physical presence, without it he was substantially diminished, a reduced power.

"I can't tell you where..."

"No, well, until you can..." We were jousting, seeing who could wrestle the impetus.

"I need to know some stuff. If you can tell me the answers I'm ready to give up, to give myself up."

"What is it you need to know?" He said wearily. Somehow Macaulay had me begging for his time and his favours.

"Blake Dukes. Our friend from Oxford. I think we killed him, but I can't be sure. And Ali. I need to know he's safe."

"A real friend, young Blake. I suppose that question means he's not with you."

I paused. I assumed he meant Ali, not Blake. I realised that Blake could be assumed missing with us rather than lying rotting in a canal basin? No, I remembered, that cannot be; he would have been mentioned on the news. Unless they were hushing that up I supposed. But all these 'what ifs were driving me crazy. I decided to not give too much away, to play it cool. "We all split up, by accident. I'm on my own now."

"I see. I'll see what I can do to get you the information you need. But I will need my pound of flesh in return. Quid pro quo, Richard. Do you know that expression?"

"I think so. It means give and take."

"Very good, Richard. That's exactly what it means. Give and take."

And then the line went dead and I replaced the receiver, slightly puzzled. A portrait of Richard and Irene stared me down. They were standing in front of a series of ornate fountains sparkling in Mediterranean sun. Although they smiled, somewhere in their faces was hard accusation. What are you doing in our house? I didn't have an answer. I felt my arm and my ribs, testing my strength. Both were much better. Would Macaulay find out what I needed to know? And how would he let me know? Somehow he had the initiative now; yet again, he had the power.

I glanced at the accusatory photo again. All right, all right, I told them. I will be gone soon.

I emptied the house of food, cooked all the rice and pasta and gobbled the contents of glass jars of nuts and raisins. I willed my injuries to mend, so I could get on the bike and escape.

It was seven o'clock and it was Thursday. Time for Top of the Pops. First up, *Do Anything You Wanna Do*. Again. The question remained: what was it exactly I wanted to do? I would have liked to hear the family TV chiming in with mine again but I couldn't ring home just for that and I had nothing to say to Mum or Beth, yet. I felt a stab of guilt. We're all worried sick, Beth had said. God knows, I thought, Mum doesn't deserve more to worry about. Maybe a call, just to say I'm all right, nothing more. And maybe they could tell me about Blake, maybe. I stared dumbly at Legs and Co gyrating to Way Down, the dead king's final song, and then, as Noel Edmonds cued The Boomtown Rats and their pantomime goofing began, I called home again.

"Hello?" Beth.

"It's Richard."

"Christ. Don't hang up this time."

"Can I speak with Mum?"

"Where are you, Richard?"

"I can't come home yet. I've just called to let mum know I'm OK."

Mum arrived on the end of the line.

"Richard." Almost a whisper.

"It's OK, mum. I won't be long."

And then I put the phone down.

The Boomtown Rats finished up and Noel Edmonds introduced Denise Williams, on video this time, and I stared listlessly at the screen for a while. At the end there was a tiny gap, a moment of silence, after the end of the song and before the cheers from the studio audience started up. But in that tiny gap I heard a minute shift behind me.

I rolled over blankly on the carpet and saw a pair of train-ers standing in the doorway, immaculate white and evenly laced. I knew straight away who these belonged to and I knew straight away what a fool I had been. My eyes travelled up Macaulay's body, the grey corduroys that swished on mead-ows, the open green bomber jacket revealing a splash of or-ange lining and finally the strong jaw, the cruel, deep-set eyes framed by tight, vigorous curls. He held my belt by his side, by the buckle, the thick black leather dangling menacingly, still but holding the threat of violence, the terror he had been waiting so long to inflict.

"Richard, finally we meet again." The bully, the authority figure, the sadistic exacter of justice was back, sure of him-self again, playful and cocky. I stared blankly at him, open mouthed.

"How did...?"

"Oh Richard, give me some credit. I'm a policeman, or I used to be." He shrugged as if that was explanation enough for his presence. An ex-policeman. Worse somehow. I guessed he had gotten in the same way I had. I felt my nerves subside. This is it, I thought. This man would deliver the truth about Blake and if he wanted me, now he had me. What's the worst thing that can happen? "I've been working hard for you, call-ing all the Mortimers in the phone book, finding out the in-formation you need..."

I sat up, trying to regain my composure. "You know what happened to Blake?"

His voice was calm. "Easy little Richard, easy does it. We have a deal, remember? Quid pro quo."

He crossed the lounge, passing me still sprawled on the floor, closed the curtains and, with a contemptuous glance at Noel Edmonds surrounded by girls in the TOTP studio, took a seat in an armchair opposite me, tapped out a Players and lit up carefully. This was the way he worked, I realised, grotesque threats of violence interspersed with calm, conciliatory chat. Gently, he put the belt down beside him.

"The Mortimers," he said, looking thoughtfully around at his surroundings, "the people who live here. Who are they? You know them?"

I shook my head.

"They keep an ashtray?" He nodded briefly at the grey ash cylinder accumulating at his cigarette's end.

"I don't know."

"As I came in I noticed a tall glass fronted cabinet. In there, I think, Mrs. Mortimer will keep an ashtray. Bottom shelf, to the left. Neither of them smoke but they will keep one there for guests." He looked me up and down carefully. "Go and get it for me. Don't make a run for it. I can hear you from here remember, walking to the cabinet and back." He toggled two fingers on an upside down hand to indicate a relaxed walk. "If you break for it..." He slowly closed the hand into a fist, angling the cigarette upwards in his other hand slightly to prevent the pillar of ash spilling. "Anyway, you won't be going. I have what you wanted: news of young Blake Dukes."

I obediently fetched his ashtray – it was exactly where Macaulay said it would be, a large, circular, cut glass affair – and held it out to Macaulay like a waiter. He tapped his ash into it and then took it carefully, sizing up its weight and sharp edges. He propped it on an armrest and smoked steadily, looking at me with the half interest and mild disgust of a sea fisherman looking at a curious deep water catch.

"Thought about running though didn't you, Richard? Despite what I said, you thought you might have a chance at a bolt. I mean you got away before, didn't you?" I nodded neutrally, not wanting to inflame his rage. "And that's not all, is it Richard?" He pointed at the ashtray. "Tell me about the ashtray."

Macaulay's games. I felt my patience straining, despite my fear. "Tell me about Blake," I said.

"Blake Dukes," he said matter-of-factly, "fell into the canal a week or so ago. Couldn't swim..." He paused and I waited for more but he was teasing me, enjoying the moment. "The ashtray," he said again.

"I thought about cracking you across the forehead with it, knocking you out cold, getting away again."

He smiled in deep satisfaction. "Of course you did, nasty piece of work that you are. But I would have been ready for you."

"What happened to Blake?"

"His brother, George, another friend of yours?" I shrugged. "George ran for help, couldn't swim either. Found a couple of students, sportsmen in training, on the towpath."

I felt a stab of guilt. Why hadn't we run for help? Blake may have been our enemy but we had left him to die.

"Did they find him? Did they get him out?"

Macaulay looked at me levelly. "Quid pro quo, Richard."

"What do you mean?"

"I mean we said give and take. But I'm doing all the giving."

"What do you want from me?"

Macaulay looked pleased at the power he held. He showed no sign of getting up, let alone attacking me. Instead he settled back in the chair, toying absently with my belt buckle. "When I was your age, life was simple. There were good people and bad people. Now..." His eyes had clouded over slightly. He stared not at me then but into the mid-distance, at a point somewhere above and to the right of my head. "My father was a policeman you know, worked a London beat, in the years after the war."

I nodded ever so slightly, noticing the tension disappear from his face; he looked relaxed, ready to open up. But I took in the ashtray too and thought about other weapons around the house, the power tools, the set of golf clubs.

"Do you know what it's like to be frightened, Richard?" I

nodded again, ever so slightly, and he gave me a look which was nearly compassionate. "Yes. I think you do. And so do I. Every night, in our little house in Shepherds Bush, I would wait in terror for the sound of my dad's boots coming up the street. The key in the lock, then the questions. Been a good boy? Done your school work? Not cheeked your mother? And every time, the voice rising, my mother crying, begging him not to do it and then..."

Macaulay trailed off. He looked absently at me then smiled again, but this time the smile was gruesome. His eyes sparked wickedly. "Violence is like a drug, Richard. My father administered it to me as a child, like a dose of bad medicine, and I've spent my life passing it on."

"What did he do?"

"He'd beat me. Drag me away from my mother, into the dining room, which was for visitors, except we never had any, so it was the beating room. He would pull up a chair and tell me, take your trousers down. He had a belt too, like yours, and he used that to tan my backside. And when he was done, and I was reduced, reduced to nothing, then we would eat, eat together as a family."

Why was he telling me this? Some crazy preamble to the violence he had promised to visit on me. But the talk seemed to be calming him. His cigarette was smouldering slowly in the ashtray, forgotten; his palms lay flat on the arms of the chair.

"I know," I said as gently as I could. "What happened to Blake, Mr. Macaulay?"

"Ah yes, quid pro quo. You want your side of the bargain. The boy lived." He delivered the verdict casually, as someone might relay a half forgotten football score. I felt a rush of excitement break through my fear. Innocent! Ali is innocent and so am I. Not guilty. Not guilty!

"How?" Despite the circumstances, the smell of violence in the room, an incredulous grin of delight had crept onto my face.

"He was under water for three minutes maximum, struggling for life on the bottom of the lock. Where you'd left him for dead." I opened my mouth to protest but decide not to interrupt. "The students, fit guys, rugby players, pulled him out and brought him round."

"Why didn't he die?"

"The rule of three, Richard. People can survive three weeks without food, three days without water, three minutes without..."

"Oxygen?" He nodded. Relief rushed over me. "You've seen him?"

"Oh yes, and his brother."

I imagined Blake, pulled from the depths of the lock by the strong arms of the sportsmen. They pumped his chest and he coughed, violently vomiting canal water onto the towpath beside him. George stood in awkward attendance embarrassed at the downfall of his brother. Then I saw Blake in the ambulance on the way to hospital, the paramedics monitoring his progress but they could see he's going to be fine; his breath rose and fell easily, his expression bore the usual cold intelligence. Finally I imagined Macaulay catching up with and interrogating Blake and George. Despite myself, I smiled at the thought. He must have scared the shit out of them.

But Macaulay was off again, talking as if to himself, lost in his past.

"...my father. The minute I left school and went to training college, he stopped knocking me about. I was fit and strong and meanwhile he was shrinking, getting weaker. I looked at him across the dinner table every night as my mother served our food, seeing the balance altering, the changing of the guard. I'd thought for a while he might be knocking mum about. Her shaking, her timidity, it all seemed to suggest she was afraid of him but I never saw anything." He paused to light a second cigarette. "Until I did..."

"What happened?"

Macaulay had a faraway look in his eyes now. All the natural light had leaked out of the sky outside and the only light was coming from the TV, a sort of static blue wash. There was another punk band on. Looking through Gary Gilmore's eyes, looking through Gary Gilmore's eyes, they shouted. Who is Gary Gilmore? I thought. And how, why, could you look through his eyes? Macaulay was made of shadow now, a hulking lump of darkness squeezed into the armchair. "I dropped round on a Thursday. Not my usual routine. I was married by then you see. Newly married actually, supposed to be in wedded bliss." His voice was heavy with sarcasm. The lit end of his fag glowed ferociously as he drew more smoke. I could just make out the firm boxer's jaw and the heavy, accusatory eyes. "Anyway I knocked at my parents' door. I had a key but they weren't expecting me and ... I killed him Richard."

We were both silent for half a minute or so.

"How?" I said finally. Echoes of Wild Bill's confession rang round my head.

Never forgot it. I could feel the whole skull give way under my fist.

A symmetry. Of sorts.

The Adverts – that was the name of the band - repeated the killer refrain. Looking through Gary Gilmore's eyes, looking through Gary Gilmore's eyes. Macaulay was telling me how he did it. Telling me about finding his mother terrified while his father lashed out with his belt, he told me about pulling his father round by the shoulder, the startled expression on his father's face freezing as his heart fails, how his mother and him watched him crumble onto the floor and how they did nothing, said nothing, not ever, until now. But I was only half listening. I would not carry their ghosts, their demons into the future. I was free, free of guilt, free to rescue my friend and bring us home.

Macaulay cleared his throat. "What I did to you, what I

tried to do to you, on the meadow, it comes from that."

I let the music play for a while longer. "And what do you want to do now?" I couldn't keep a hint of mockery, of contempt, out of my voice.

Then suddenly he was on his feet. He grabbed the belt and made for me. I felt a burning lash against my shoulder, my good shoulder. Then his muscular arms had me and he pulled me onto my feet and gave me a slap first one way and then the other across my chops.

"Come on Richard," he brayed, a hideous grin spreading across his face, "Come on!"

He wanted me to fight back and I tried, punching his stomach lamely. It fell ineffectually on a wall of muscle. In response he delivered a punch, a right-hander that sent me sprawling into the chair where minutes earlier Macaulay had been delivering his confession. My hand hit hard glass. The ashtray: it was waiting for us all along. We both knew it.

Float, float on, went the TV. Macaulay reached down to pull me up by the shoulders again and I let him have it, straight across the forehead with the curved edge of the ashtray. Like a discus thrower throwing into the distance.

And Macaulay fell.

Not dead, not even out. He shouted out in gruesome, twisted pain.

And I stood over him, shouting back. "It's over now," I told him," No more. No more quid pro quo."

He stopped shouting. He was nodding slowly. He took his hands away from his forehead and revealed the blood, a nasty gash there. But I knew he would live. He would live.

"I won't pass it on," I told him, finding strength and resolution from somewhere and surprising myself with the conviction in my voice. "The fighting stops here. It stops right here."

And then I was out, on the bike, cycling furiously away in the near dark. No lights but I didn't care. I crossed the river and saw a sign for Windsor. 14 miles to Windsor. I rode as hard as I could, ignoring the pain in my sore arm and ribs, and now from the belt lash too. I saw headlights in the distance and for a moment imagined the Hillman and its crazed driver in pursuit, blood oozing from his wounded forehead. But I knew he wouldn't come after me now and even if he did I wouldn't be afraid. I was not afraid of anyone anymore, not Blake, not Macaulay, not anyone.

Hare Hatch, another sleepy village. Large front gardens, adorned with expensive cars. A space between the front fence and the hedge. One more night sleeping rough. I gathered my jumper around me. Singing to myself, to the tune of Tiger Feet.

Blake lives.
Blake lives.
Blake lives.
Blake lives.
Blake lives.
Blake lives.
Blake lives.

Twenty-one

VIKRAM

First light I pulled the Mortimer's racer out of the bush and got back on the road. I followed the signs to Windsor and soon saw the castle rising above the tidy terraces and orange new builds. The sun was back again, bouncing hot and bright off the walls and towers of the castle and spotlighting the streets as it flooded through from the east.

I reached a row of shops: a butcher's, a small cafe and baby clothes outlet. The question was how to find where the travelers were holed up. I pushed the racer past the row of shops and found a grubby looking newsagent at the end. At the shop's side was an alley and I propped the racer up at the back behind some bins out of sight.

I pushed open a heavy door, a bell chimed and a squat Indian man with a gleaming, shiny crown and tufts of wiry silver fuzz sprouting from his nose and ears looked up from his newspaper. This would not work, I realised, this man won't know where to find a traveler's site. But he was looking at me alertly, keenly. Something of the bulldog in him, a shrewd, indomitable spirit that suggested Winston Churchill. "Good morning. How may I help you?" Cut glass English, another surprise.

"I'm looking for a travelers' site. Somewhere near here."

"A travelers' site, you say?" A bushy eyebrow rose and deep brown eyes assessed me gently.

"It's my friend. He's with them. At least I think he is. And I have news for him, something important."

"News, you say?" The eyes scanned me. Not penetrating, not interrogative, but wise, thorough and exacting. I saw a quick and logical mind calculating, connecting and surmising. Finally, he released a benign smile. "Two boys, Richard Turner and Alistair Johnston, missing from the city of Oxford some 10 days ago. Spotted in Reading once, but otherwise remaining invisible, keeping out of reach of the authorities." He nodded at the newspaper beneath his elbows. "I keep an eye on the news."

He had me at his mercy. A phone call and I was finished. "I would hazard that you are Richard Turner, the younger of the two. You have followed the Thames and now you are in Windsor. A logical progression. You are seeking Alistair Johnston. And you think you will find him with a group of travelling people. Yes, maybe you will." He slid off the stool on which he had been perched and surprisingly reduced in height. Standing up, he was a good six inches smaller than me, tiny for a fully- grown man. Then he turned and bellowed something in a foreign language into the doorway leading to the interior behind the shop that sounded like 'lack sea.' A bright-eyed urchin in an electric blue tunic appeared, "My daughter, Lakshmi," he said and volleyed some instructions at the girl. Then he beckoned me. "Come on, come through, come through."

I hesitated. This could be a trap. Maybe he wanted to be in the newspapers himself, responsible for delivering a lost boy into the hands of the law. But I doubted it. There was something in his countenance that demanded faith, belief in his ability to help and his sincerity. I passed the impishly grinning daughter and went through a bead curtain into a store room with cellophane wrapped boxes and cartons stacked in neat piles, then into a small square room with floor cushions where the walls were plastered with posters of lurid, hallucinogenic

Indian gods, a man with an elephant head and a woman with a head full of snakes. He waved me graciously to the floor and I took a seat awkwardly on the cushions. The air smelt strongly of spices.

I remembered my bike and gabbled a concern. Wordlessly, he let himself out of a back door and I caught a glimpse of white metal as he pulled my bike into his back yard. "Bicycle is safe," he said simply.

I caught a glimpse of a stout, coffee-coloured ankle with a silver bracelet in an adjoining kitchen.

"Abha, chai accha," said my bulldog. A singsong reply in Hindi from the kitchen. "Tea is coming," he told me solemnly.

"Thank you. I didn't catch your name."

"Then I will throw it at you for you to catch." He grinned. The same smile as his daughter. "My name is Vikram." Another shy grin. "Tell me your story."

So I did. I told him the entire tale, no edits, no embellishments, no exaggeration: the trains, Blake and the canal, Macaulay, Brenna and the travelers, Wild Bill, the whole lot. At one point, an almost perfectly spherical woman in a green sari, brought a tray with two curious metal cups and a jug of sweet, spiced tea but I didn't stop talking; it was as if I was unburdening, spilling out the whole thing so it didn't belong to me anymore. At the end Vikram nodded gravely.

"Quite a tale. Through your life, you will tell this again and again, and over time it will sharpen into a saga to rival the Mahabharata." That grin again, another flash of pearly whites. "And so, for the story's conclusion we need two things. Your message to reach Alistair and you to go home to your waiting family. Is this correct?"

I nodded hesitantly. But it was right, it was correct.

Vikram continued. "The traveler site you seek, it is in an area of woodland not far from here. What you need to know is how to get to your friend, perhaps without attracting the attention of the leader, this Arthur Maguire, and maybe also this Brenna Maguire and her sciurine younger brother. Correct again?"

I nod. Sci-irine? I had no idea what he was talking about but I knew I had met a man who was clearly intelligent and had been fortunate to find him too. "How did you know where the camp is?" I asked.

In explanation, Vikram pointed to a local newspaper sitting folded on the table. "Nothing like this goes unobserved in these parts. And I know this area. There is somewhere I can take you to. I can drop you in my van where you can access a path through the woods. If you are careful, the foliage will conceal you and prevent detection but at the same time afford you a good view of the camp. It will be my pleasure to help you because your cause is ultimately an honourable one. But, speaking of honour, there is the question of a debt to be repaid..."

"The bike?"

"Quite so. The damage to the house will no doubt be accounted for by an insurance claim. I would neglect to mention it when the police catch up with you. The bicycle, I shall ensue is returned to the Mortimers."

I nodded and smiled in thanks. And Vikram returned my nod solemnly and closed his eyes for a second, a gesture acknowledging my gratitude and signalling his humility.

Leaving Vikram's family behind, we climbed into his battered transit and picked our way through Windsor. We crossed the river and suddenly there were kids in black tail coats and stiff, high white collars everywhere, crossing the road, talking in huddles, marching four abreast along the pavements.

"Students of Eton College," said Vikram, wryly, "tomorrow's politicians, bankers, business men perhaps. Soon they will be commencing their studies once more, learning how to rule the world."

I looked at the groups of sharp-eyed boys, moving imperiously towards a giant chapel surrounded by minaret-like towers. The boys looked at once the same and different from my school intake. And suddenly I pictured the crowds of lads in Oxford converging on Walton Boys for the new term, my lads, my people. They were gathered together in groups, catching up after the summer, running fingers through new bristly haircuts, treading on each other's squeaky new shoes. The main topic on their lips? The prime summer gossip? Richard Turner and Ali Johnston, runaways, lost to the wilds, maybe dead. And nobody knows where, or why? Except maybe...

Blake and George Dukes arrive almost unnoticed, slipping past the crowds just before the first bell of the new school year spilled across the concrete apron inside the gates. Blake left George at the huts and took his seat quietly at the back of 5D where he answered neutrally and correctly when his form teacher called his name. The summer was over and he had plans on his mind, joining the army, getting far away, shaking off the confines of his parents and brother for good. Some of the boys sitting in front of him had heard he might have had something to do with the missing boys; they'd heard they were friends with the Dukes brothers maybe, fell out, had a fight perhaps. But no one asked him. Blake was not the sort of lad you would ask something like that, not straight out. He was quiet, kept himself to himself, one of the lads but then again not really. In the hubbub of the new term beginning, his connection with the runaways was soon forgotten, as indeed were the runaways themselves.

But George Dukes, arriving in the hut to take his seat in 4R, noting the idiot alphabet posters and nursery colour scheme was unchanged from last year, was not so unapproachable, not feared, not so separate.

"George," hissed Jamie Malloy, lolling sideways in his chair, bottom lip hanging baggily beneath an array of crooked teeth, "George, did you kill that Turner kid? And Ali Johnston?"

George's face remained as blank as always. He had nothing for Malloy or anyone else. He trotted out the party line. "Don't know anything about it," he said smugly, "got nothing to do with us."

Vikram's van left the city and headed out across fields, before reaching the outskirts of what looked like a village. Vikram pointed towards a field dotted with the parched remains of some harvested crops and, beyond that, a wood, giant oaks and elms stretching upwards, topmost leaves caught in a wind blowing firmly towards us.

"That is your way Richard," said Vikram softly, indicating the dense foliage at the foot of the trees. I followed where his finger was pointing and thought I could see a way in, an entrance into the green.

"I see it."

He nodded and raised a bushy eyebrow quizzically. I nodded back with as much formality as I could manage. I had a strong urge to hug him, maybe even kiss his cheek, to thank this wise, warm, kind man with my heart as well as my head but instead all he got was another idiot grin as I spilt awkwardly out onto the pavement.

I blinked in the sunlight, taking in my surroundings. A neat row of post-war semis; tidy front gardens; all quiet apart from the steady burr of traffic from a nearby overhead bridge. I made my way away from the houses, along the edge of a field towards the woods. Once inside, I could see a path running through the wood's centre but I branched off it as soon as I could, making my way to the thickest, bushiest part where the trees hung low and the brambles coiled up towards my thighs. I was moving slowly, mindful of Squirrel's artistry. This time I wanted to see them before they saw me. And soon enough I caught a white wall ahead - a truck's side - and, beyond it, I glimpsed people moving around. There were around a dozen vans, a smallish site in defensive mode. Their doors opened onto a central clearing with a large, dead fire area surrounded by the open backs of the trucks huddled close together, shutting off the world.

Staying in the cover of the bushes, I moved slowly round the edge of a large truck in order to get a better view. Soon I found a vantage point where I could see, through a gap between two trucks, travelers moving to and from their vehicles, carrying wood or sitting smoking in the sun. I dropped into a ditch where I could lie down full length and pull old bark and leaves over my body for camouflage. Then I glimpsed Arthur lurch across the site, calling cheerfully to his dogs, and felt a shiver of fear and excitement. I had tracked them down! I was exactly where I wanted to be and I had got there through my own industry. Ali, I thought, I know you are there and I am taking you home.

And there he was! Ali moved across the main clearing following Arthur. He had dumped the clothes he had been wearing when we escaped - his jeans, jacket and Leeds scarf. Now he wore a long sleeved black T-shirt and clumsy army boots, obviously acquired from his new family. He looked every inch the travelling boy, one of Arthur's own. I felt a sting then: Arthur had accepted him but wouldn't take me. Ali moved out of sight and I shimmied out of the hollow and crawled under a truck to try and get a better look. Above me was the rusty apparatus of the truck, the rods and pipes were inches from my head. The trouble was that there I had an even worse view of the camp than I had in the ditch; all I could see was boots and paws. Paws. Dogs. They would surely notice me soon, I realised with alarm. Maybe only the wind blowing from behind the camp was saving me, keeping my scent away from the hounds.

"Alright?" Unmistakably Arthur's voice, clear rogue authority, shot through with a strain of matey affection. I matched his army boots to the voice. They were laced only loosely at the bottom so he could slip them off easily when he got into his truck. One was above the other as he sat easily by the fire, cross-legged, a general ready to issue orders from his centre of operations. "Keepin' y'ead down I 'ope?"

"Yes Arthur." Ali. His boots were new and laced to the top, ready for action. They stood deferentially a few feet off Arthur.

"Wood pile's getting low again," said Arthur casually.

A dog growled and I froze. One of Arthur's hounds, an Alsatian, fussed at his feet. If it had come for me under the truck it would have savaged my face and I wouldn't have been able to do much to defend myself. It fretted, pushing its nose to the ground, straining for the scent, my scent, it had caught, but not knowing where it came from. The wind continued towards me; I could see it lifting the grass. Then we made eye contact, the dog and I - I swear we did. The dog growled again but I held its gaze, willing him to accept me, to hold off.

"Easy boy," said Arthur. He ruffled the dog's collar. I edged backwards, holding the dog's eyes. I was reminded of the fox in the woods. Hey boy, I mouthed, easy boy.

"I'll get some more wood," said Ali.

"You do that," said Arthur. Ali's boots headed off, in the direction of the woods on the other side of the camp. Now I had a chance to intercept him.

I wriggled backwards and began to move around the edge of the camp, carefully picking my way through the brambles and bushes. All the time, I kept my eyes rooted on the camp, looking hard for a sign that anyone had noticed me. I could hear Arthur at the camp's centre, calling out cheerfully to his people and his dogs. I guessed as I moved around the back of the trucks that the dogs would pick up my scent. I needed to get to Ali fast, before the hounds could reach me.

I moved round the camp. I was making some noise now but I didn't care. Then the woods opened into a clearing and there was Ali, pulling aimlessly at the branches of a rotten trunk, trying to salvage something combustible. I was about to call out his name when barking exploded from the direction of the camp's centre. They had picked up my scent and would be on me in seconds.

I called out to Ali and he looked up startled from his aimless wood collecting.

"You've got to call the dogs off me," I said.

"Rich. Jesus."

Then we both turned towards the camp's centre again because we heard Arthur growl out a challenge. Someone had arrived at the camp. So the dogs were not interested in me after all. But I could guess who the visitor was. Macaulay: like some desperate drowning man, he couldn't let go, wouldn't give up. Brenna and Squirrel crashed through the trees towards us from the same direction.

"Rich!" said Brenna, as surprised as I had ever seen her. And the four of us were standing marvelling at one another in the clearing, all smiling, even Squirrel. But there was no time. "You've got to be off," said Brenna urgently to Ali, "some bloke's here, weirdo, could be a copper. He's asking for you. You know what Arthur says..."

Ali looked at me. I was all he had got.

"He's coming with me," I said and Brenna and Squirrel looked at me, surprised by my strength of feeling. "Ali didn't kill that boy," I told them urgently, "they pulled him out of the lock. He's alive. He's alright." I turned to Ali who was looking at me incredulously. "He's all right Ali. Blake's alive and well."

I saw a weight lift off my friend's shoulders. His eyes brightened, but he was still not sure. "What ... how? How do you know?"

"Macaulay, he told me. And he's not a policeman, he's a ... he's dangerous." Voices were raised in the clearing. He would be with us soon. "He's here now," I told Brenna, "that's him. He doesn't give up. Thought I'd seen the last..."

There was a noise from the woods behind Brenna and Squirrel. "They're coming for you," said Brenna, "go. I'll stop him coming after you." I looked at Ali. He was looking searchingly at Brenna but she flashed him a grin and urged him away. "Go on murder boy, time to go."

He grinned. "Maybe not murder boy after all."

And she smiled back, at both of us.

We turned to leave, to set off again. Ali and me on the run again just like before, a winning team, a survival machine. And this time we were going home. Like conquering heroes we would line up for school again but we had changed, grown, become men. No one could catch us; they never could. Maybe we would go home now but maybe we would spend one last night out, in the wilds, because we could, because...

Mr. Steven Johnston arrived in the clearing. There was no sign of Macaulay.

I stopped, frozen, disarmed by the tender, searching eyes of Ali's dad. Suddenly I was back in Reading and in the moment I noticed Ali had stopped behind me outside the pub, his dad oblivious to his presence. And then, although I was beside my friend, I was 50 yards apart from him once more. He was cutting me loose again: this time Ali's dad had come to take him home.

Mr. Johnston was dressed as he was that day: jeans, black shoes, a leather bomber jacket, his hair cut short and shot with grey through the temples, but this time his face opened into a smile of delight and relief. He had found his son. Behind him, Arthur grinned too, pleased to facilitate the reunion.

Ali moved towards his dad.

I stepped uncertainly backwards and folded myself against the trunk of a tree, not sure what to do. I felt hot tears arrive behind my eyes and dismissed them angrily. Cry baby! And what for? Ali had found his dad and Mr. Johnston had found his son. What right did I have to be upset or angry about that?

I saw Brenna and Squirrel creep away too, lurking at the edge of clearing. They found a place in the shadow of a tree in which to stand respectfully off, to quietly observe the reunion too. Arthur stopped and let Mr. Johnston go to his son alone.

"Where have you been?" I heard Mr. Johnston say.

Ali shrugged. He looked at the floor. "Here and there," is what I think he said. Then he said something else to Mr. Johnston and called out, to me and then to Brenna and Squirrel and we converged on Ali's dad. He solemnly offered up his hand and thanked solemnly in turn.

"You're Richard," he said, "I'm so glad you're safe too. You've got people at home very worried about you."

"Thank you for looking after my son," he said to Arthur. Suddenly we all looked like little children, even Brenna.

"He's a good lad," said Arthur simply.

There was an awkward silence. I realised everyone was looking at Ali in a different way, seeing him as a different person. Mr. Johnston saw his lost son, his little boy; Brenna and Squirrel were adjusting to the new Ali, murder boy no longer, a boy with roots, a home. And I was looking at my friend and thinking how we had grown, how the two of us took on the wilds and how we had come out with adults, Arthur and Mr. Johnston, quietly wishing us well.

Eventually Mr. Johnston said we had better go; he reminded us that our mothers in Oxford would be waiting; they would be delighted to welcome us home. Arthur gave us a quick grin and a nod and disappeared into the folds of his camp. He had already got other things on his mind: the next journey, the next scraps of work, the next camp. Brenna watched him go. She looked awkward, finally she was the child she should be, like all of us. Squirrel hid behind her.

"I'll come and see you," said Ali to Brenna and he looked at me a bit helplessly. "Rich too," he added.

I nodded earnestly but I knew it was not true. Brenna had let us, Ali really, into her world but now she saw there was another side to us, a normal life of towns and schools, she was letting us go, forever.

She shrugged. "Yeah, 'course," she said simply. She smiled briefly.

And then they were gone and we walked back towards Mr. Johnston's Renault and headed back towards Oxford. Ali sat in the front of the car and I took the back seat. I kept seeing glimpses of our journey to Windsor out of the window: hedges, railways, canals, rivers. The three of us were silent. There was too much to think about, too much adjustment.

Mr. Johnston pulled the car onto a lay-by a few miles outside Oxford. I could see the flat plain of the Thames valley ahead, the towers at Didcot, the tapestry of field and woodland, the way home.

"Look," he said, "when we get back, they'll be all sorts of fuss and your mothers will be all over you and maybe the police and well … I'll kind of disappear…"

Ali started to protest but Mr. Johnston raised his hand. "No, don't worry. Not for long, not this time, but I wanted to say, while I've got the chance … When you left I realised I had to do better. I couldn't believe you had come to find me and I hadn't helped you. I ran after you Rich, with the others, trying to catch, but you were too fast for me, too fast for all of us." He gave me a wry smile. "But I knew then I had to find you and I'm bloody glad I did. Both of you."

"But how did you find us dad?" Asked Ali.

"Looked hard and didn't stop. I got nowhere for two days, three days. Coppers were no help. Told me to leave it to them. Even though they had no idea where you'd gone. My hunch was wrong. I thought you'd track back up the river towards Oxford so I walked the river that way, asking everyone I met on the way. Everyone. Someone must know something I thought. Then finally I struck lucky. A lonesome cowboy, of all people!"

"Wild Bill." Ali and I exchanged an affectionate smile.

"Yes that's him. Met him right outside Oxford, him and a bunch of drinking buddies, all stinking drunk and stinking dirty too..."

"Bill told you where I was?" Ali sounded surprised and almost a little disappointed in this transgression of the outlaws' code.

"No he didn't," said Mr. Johnston, "at least not directly although God knows I bought the four of them enough booze to loosen the tongues of an army of war prisoners. Wild Bill said he'd seen you two but he wouldn't or couldn't tell me anything else. You haven't been with him have you? I could never work out if he was telling the truth."

"Sort of," said Ali.

"What they wouldn't shut up about was a boy they said had drowned in the lock, right where they were, in the water in front of them..."

"Blake..." I muttered.

"Yes, well I found out that was nonsense. The boy was rescued by some students although it was a close thing according to a policeman I met..." This time I didn't say anything. "A DS Macaulay. He was very anxious to find you. Not like the other coppers. He took my number and gave me his. Very keen to find you two, he was, especially you, Rich. Anyway Bill gave me one thing, a name - Little Brenna - and a load of other nonsense besides but that name led me to Arthur Maguire eventually and to you two."

"But how did you find out where Ali was with just a name? Brenna's name?" I asked.

"Macaulay. Two nights ago he rang me very excited. Said he was close to tracking you down Richard, said you'd called him and given a family name but no address. He asked me if I knew the name Mortimer. When I said I didn't, he told me he would be able to trace you soon. But he said you weren't with Richard, Ali, and I felt sort of desperate so I started throwing all the nonsense Wild Bill had come out with at Macaulay in the hope something might stick. When I said the name Brenna, he said it sounded Irish and that it was a long shot but a bunch of travelers, a lot of them Irish, had been moved on by the police from a site near Radley a week or so back and they were led by a man named Arthur Maguire who might well be in a new site now, near Windsor!"

Ali and I smiled at each other and Mr. Johnston caught it. "So how did you get mixed up with Macaulay?" he asked.

We laughed. "He thought I owed him something," I said, "but it got settled."

Mr. Johnston grinned. "Well, there's a tale there I'm sure. I didn't like him much, I've got to say. He seemed obsessed with finding Richard and almost not bothered about you, Ali, which annoyed me. Still anyone who could help me..."

We left it there and drove into Oxford. I felt calm, ready to go home, ready to climb into my favourite armchair and watch TV. Since Ali had found his dad, something had settled inside me, a righting of wrongs, and a falling into place of lost pieces. *I need to find my dad.* He had always said it. And he had been right. As for me, I knew I won't ever find my dad but I knew then I could get along fine without one. Ali and I had taken the world on and had done a lot of growing up but funnily enough growing up had made me want to be a boy again, a boy from Jericho, Oxford with a school and a family, annoying sisters and a lovely mum. But I had seen the world, struck out on my own. I was happy with that.

They left me at the corner and I walked up my street and let myself in the through the back like I always did. The smell of sausages filled the yard.

"Mum," I shouted, "I'm home!"

John B Bliss is a crime writer from Brighton, UK. His writing explores society's seedy underbelly: the derelict and forgotten characters left at the margins. The Murder Boys is his first full-length novel and he is currently working on a sequel.

Word-of-mouth is essential for any author to succeed.
If you enjoyed The Murder Boys, please consider leaving a review on Amazon.
Even a couple of lines would make a difference and would be extremely appreciated.

If you enjoyed **The Murder Boys** you may want to check
out other exciting books on our website:
http://www.crimewavepress.com
Subscribe to our newsletter and you will be amongst the first
to learn about new **Crime Wave Press** titles and
free advance readers copies.

Crime Wave Press is a Hong Kong based fiction imprint
that endeavors to publish some of the best new
crime novels from around the world.

Founded in 2012 by acclaimed publisher Hans Kemp of
Visionary World and seasoned writer Tom Vater,
Crime Wave Press publishes a range of crime fiction –
from whodunits to Noir and Hardboiled,
from historical mysteries to espionage thrillers,
from literary crime to pulp fiction,
from highly commercial page turners to
marginal texts exploring life's dark underbelly.

Follow us on Facebook:
http://www.facebook.com/CrimeWavePress

Printed in Great Britain
by Amazon